Cameron's Contract

An Enthrall Novella

Vanessa Fewings

Cameron's Contract
Copyright © 2015 Vanessa Fewings

This story is a work of fiction. References to real people, events, establishments, organizations, or locales are intended only to provide a sense of authenticity and are used fictitiously. All other characters, and all incidents and dialogue are drawn from the author's imagination and are not to be construed as real.

Cover design by VMK
Cover photo is by Zigroup-Creations from Shutterstock

Book formatted and edited by Louise Bohmer:
http://www.louisebohmer.com/site/freelance/

Paperback ISBN: 978-0-9965014-7-7
Ebook ISBN: 978-0-9912046-6-3

DEDICATION

For Louise Bohmer, my wonderful editor, and for Mary, Debbie, and Diane.

"Before the beginning of great brilliance, there must be chaos."

I Ching

CHAPTER 1

DUKKHA.

This Buddhist term loosely translates into the word suffering, a feeling of being unsettled, or off kilter.

To be free of dukkha, one is advised to behave decently, not act on impulse, and function mindfully. The opposite of this best described me right now, with my grip tight around the Bugatti Veyron's wheel, feeling impulsive and full of rage, with no intention of any decency.

I was going to fucking kill someone.

And the only way to end this suffering was to get Mia back— my lover, my beautiful, sweet submissive—who was driving my BMW ahead of us way too fast.

Barely twenty-one, and the most beautiful woman I'd ever known, her sweet nature miraculously remained untouched despite all she'd been through.

Shay's focus roamed from his laptop balanced on his knees, where he tracked the car, to back on the road. His intense concentration was a change from his usual humorous self, but, as my head of security and proven techno genius, he knew I was on tilt. My woman was driving into danger, and if that small red blip was correct we were about to lose her.

As an ex-SEAL, Shay wasn't a stranger to all this drama, though he did squirm when our speed hit a hundred.

I loosened my necktie, self-hate welling in my gut.

"Which one's the air conditioner?" Shay's hand hovered over the dashboard. "This looks like a flight panel."

I turned the air up for him, and weaved around the car in front.

My focus remained on not hitting any of the other cars, but evening traffic barely lightened up.

A promise had been broken.

I'd told Mia I'd protect her from the wolves and never again would anyone hurt her. Yet here she was heading into danger, willing to face off with an old enemy, and all this was to protect me. I knew this with certainty.

It started with that sinister appearance of Adrian Herron a few days ago outside Badgley Mischka. Mia refused to talk about it. My miscalculation came in not pushing her to open up about it. Now I knew without a doubt it had been him. This bastard had murdered her mother and then left a fourteen-year-old Mia to carry the guilt. Her past had caught up and I'd not seen it coming.

An innocent morning shift working at Charlie's Soup Kitchen had put Mia in jeopardy, and despite having my driver Leo watch her from inside the cafeteria, and Shay's team guarding the property from outside, Adrian's younger brother Decker had infiltrated my charity café, cloaked as a staff member. He'd gotten to Mia, and intimidated her into silence.

Decker Herron had snatched Mia's collar off her, right there in Charlie's Soup Kitchen, leaving the scar on the nape of her neck to prove it. I'd been so full of jealousy I'd missed the most importance piece of evidence. The kind that would have elicited questions and prevented Mia from ever leaving my Beverly Hills home and trying to deal with this herself. I'd believed her lie about how she'd sustained that small abrasion.

"Let's call it in." Shay glanced over at me. "Please, Cam."

"I'm handling it—"

"This should be me. My men—"

"Mia is my woman—"

"You're too invested, Cam. You're emotional right now. Understandably, but still. Will you please slow down!"

"And risk losing her?"

"It's a good idea to turn up alive."

I eased up on the gas, not least because my dashboard blinked to indicate a cop car was fifty feet ahead.

2

"Your team as well as Leo were meant to be watching her," I snapped. "No one noticed Mia enter Charlie's wearing a choker, yet when she left—"

"We fucked up." He tapped the laptop in frustration. "They're meant to make a note of every detail, including what she's wearing, incase…"

"She goes missing?"

"I don't know what happened. I'm sorry. Men will be fired. I can promise you that."

I knew what had happened.

Leo had assumed the team outside was watching Mia, and the same went for them. After all, Leo was ex-military too. With his experience, they'd assumed an ex-marine had what it took to watch over a young woman for three hours. Or so you'd have thought.

"I've let her down," I said.

"I take full responsibility." He pointed at the screen. "We're closing in on her."

"Where did she go?"

"Shit."

"She's under a bridge." I sounded calmer then I felt.

Shay refreshed the screen. And then again. "There she is. We've got her."

I let out a slow, steady breath.

"We need a gun," I said. "Have one of your men meet us there."

"If she gets to that house before us, you're not going in, Cole." My jaw tensed and I ignored him.

"She's heading off the freeway." He pointed. "Next exit."

I navigated the car across three lanes.

"I showed Mia the address of where her collar is on my phone and she committed it to memory."

"She's super smart, Shay. Everyone underestimates her. She's gone through my entire collection of books by Joseph Campbell, and she's currently obsessed with the work of Milton Erickson."

I turned left onto the street and cursed when we hit a red light, willing it to change and close to running it.

"I know you love her," Shay said.

Mercifully we got a green and I touched the gas, propelling us through the cross street.

"She's different, Shay."

"I know."

"If anything happens to her—"

"Well we taught her a few self-defense moves back in London."

"That means nothing." I gestured to the screen.

He glanced back "Behind us. Back up."

I threw the Bugatti into reverse, wheels squealing as we flew backwards.

I hit the brakes and peered over.

The BMW was parked. Headlights off.

Mia was gone.

CHAPTER 2

"WHERE THE HELL are you?" Henry's gruff voice boomed through my phone.

Through force of habit, Shay placed his hand on the BMW's hood to feel for warmth.

"Henry, where are you?" I said.

"On the plane. You?"

"An hour away."

"Where are you?"

If I told him downtown L.A., he'd know I was close. "Can I call you back?"

My gaze swept the small homes overshadowed by office buildings. City Hall loomed in view.

"You're not doing this, Cam."

"Doing what?"

"I know your feelings about Cole Tea—"

"I'm right behind you."

Shay gestured for me to cut the call.

"Get to New York," I said. "I'll catch the next flight."

"What's going on?"

"I have to go—"

"Cameron, it looks bad."

I followed Shay down a pathway between two houses. "Don't lose hope, Henry."

The phone became muffled and I heard him talking to the

pilot. My heart sunk with the realization I was letting Henry down, letting them all down.

I should've been on that flight.

"Henry, I'm as devastated as you about the business."

"Actions speak louder, Cam."

My grip tightened around my phone. "Cover for me."

A long silence fueled the tension.

"Henry?"

"I've got your back."

"I'll make it up to you."

I glanced left and right, flanked between two tall, rundown wooden fences.

"The stewardess is giving me the stink eye." He killed the call.

My feet melted into the asphalt. The air thick and the threat of rain suffocated in this muggy heat. Many of the homes had bars on the windows, which didn't bode well. Several streetlights were out.

I ached for Mia.

Shay held his phone out and followed the blip leading us to the collar. He looked back at the BMW and Bugatti Veyron, both self-indulgent contrasts to the cars around them.

Damn the cars.

Shay led the way and we continued down the alleyway. Over his shoulder, I watched that red dot. Jewelry that had put Mia in danger was ironically leading us to her now.

"There," I said in a rush.

Mia was up ahead.

She hurried toward a rundown house with bars on the windows. The shades were drawn. The lawn was long dead.

Shay grabbed my arm. "Stay here."

I broke away and sprinted toward her, blood roaring in my ears, my lungs not caring if they ever filled again. Those early morning runs paid off in a way I'd never imagined.

Mia lingered on the top step of the house. Her hand reached out to knock.

Tearing across the lawn, it felt like it took a lifetime to reach her.

She didn't see me.

I swept her up and pulled her around to the right side of the house and shoved her against the wall. My palm covered her mouth.

Her terror showed, but recognition softened her frown. Her body trembled.

She startled when Shay sprinted around the corner.

"You're probably wondering how I found you?" I whispered.

Her gaze returned to mine and she gave a nod.

I leaned in. "I shoved a bug up your ass when you were sleeping." I arched an amused brow and, despite my heart still trying to force its way out, I forced a smile.

Mia stared up at me, blinking her confusion.

Despite this relief, my mind was ablaze with the consequences of what might have happened if she'd disappeared inside. These two men had proven their violence. It pained me to think it had been me who'd driven her here.

"Cole," Shay said. "What the hell was that? I'm trying to protect you here."

Mia squeezed her eyes shut.

I ignored his glare and asked her, "What are you doing here?"

Her frown deepened as she eased my hand away. "I'm taking care of it."

"What exactly?" snapped Shay.

"Back off," I told him.

"They just want a little money," she whispered. "They promised—"

"You come to me with crap like this," said Shay.

"Mia, how can you bear to face that man after what he did to you?" I said. "To your mom?"

"He threatened you, Cameron." Her hand reached for her collar that was no longer there. "They swore they could ruin your reputation."

"They don't have that kind of power, Mia, unless you give it to them."

"But—"

"We know they have your choker."

She held back tears. "I'm going to get it back."

"Forgive me for spanking you, sweetheart," I said. "It was unconscionable."

"I let him walk away with your beautiful choker."

"You're more important. Don't ever forget that. Never put

7

yourself in danger again."

"Adrian threatened to leak my past to the press," she said. "Tell the world you're dating the daughter of a drug addict."

"Oh, Mia. What would be the worst that could happen if that came out?"

"They told me it would affect Cole Tea."

I glanced over at Shay.

We both knew Cole Tea didn't need any help nose-diving into history.

Mia wrapped her fingers around my hand. "They warned me if I told you they'd contact the press."

"Did Decker grab your collar off you this morning?" asked Shay.

She gave a nod, and she looked so worn down, so fragile.

"I'm sorry I shouted at you—" My arm shot up to protect her from the blur of movement to our left.

It was Emma, from Shay's security team. We'd witness firsthand what she was capable of outside The Manor a few days ago. Her Ronda Rousey moves were legendary. Emma had taken down my attacker so quickly no one had seen a thing until the man was lying on the floor.

She handed Shay a gun and he tucked it inside his jacket. A few maneuvers later and he'd also hooked up a wire beneath his shirt, with Emma's help.

I turned to face Mia. "Stay with Emma."

"Let me talk to him," she said.

Shay scoffed at that and tucked whatever else Emma had handed him into his jacket pocket.

"I have to deal with this," said Mia. "This is my problem."

"No, Mia," I said calmly. "They want me. And they've come after me through you. I'm going to make it go away." I wrapped an arm around her waist and led her to safety.

I forced her to sit in the car, where she'd be safe with Emma and two of Shay's guards watching over her. They'd turned up fast, making this an impressive display of his security detail. All this apparently went on in the background, and I paid Shay well not to see it.

With Mia calmed in the back of the Cadillac Escalade, Shay and I returned to the Herron's front door.

"Sure you want to do this?" he said.

I held back on this urge to kick it down. Shay had to see me calm, collected, ready to deal with them and not escalate the situation.

"Take off your tie," he said. "Less formal."

After pulling it from my neck, I tucked it into my pocket.

Shay knocked.

Fierce barking came from inside, chilling my veins and setting off my adrenaline.

Shay casually sprinkled dark crumbs along the doorstep and dropped more along the threshold.

He met my gaze. "Emma checked the pet registry on the way here." He brushed his hands together to get rid of the rest. "Dog food."

I admired his forethought. "What kind?"

"Kibbles 'n' Bits."

"I meant the dog."

He gave a shrug. "Rottweiler."

CHAPTER 3

THE PUNGENT SMELL hit us.

Dog urine and burned food and something else—cigarettes and stale beer. A TV blared from the living room, raising the stakes to the drama.

Decker stood in the open doorway staring us down.

He'd aged from his driving license photo taken five years ago. A crooked life hadn't been kind to him. He looked older than twenty-six. His boxer shorts and vest needed a wash. He hadn't shaved in a while, or combed his hair.

If my ex-girlfriend McKenzie saw this tattooed stud now, the one everyone supposedly swooned over at Charlie's, she'd have shut her damned mouth and run. To think I'd been fretting over this mystery man being a threat.

McKenzie had bitched her way beneath my skin, making me believe Mia was having an affair with this asshole, and all the while the sinister truth had loomed right in front of me. Regret seeped into my bones. I'd doubted Mia, doubted us.

Zen was called for. Not just here, now, but in the way I usually conducted my life. I'd let emotion get in the way and it had threatened all I held dear.

Fucked up everything.

That dog barked viciously from somewhere in the back of the house.

"Decker Hern?" I asked.

He went to close the door. "Not buying anything."

"You work at Charlie's?" I smiled.

His gaze swept the street behind us.

"Bad time?" said Shay.

Decker studied us. "Kind of."

"You're right." I turned away. "We should go."

"You don't want your New Year bonus?" asked Shay, surprised.

"He's busy." I tucked my hands into my pockets and turned to go. "We're running late anyway."

Shay glanced my way. His brow arched to convey what we both now new. Decker didn't know who I was.

"Sorry to have bothered you." Shay went to follow me.

"You should have called first," said Decker.

Shay turned back to him. "You didn't get the email?"

"Email?"

"That's another one," I said.

"What kind of bonus?" asked Decker.

Shay patted his jacket pocket as though looking for it. "You've got this one," he said to me.

"I've never seen you at Charlie's?" said Decker.

"We're from corporate," said Shay. "They make us troll the neighborhood and piss off employees. Nobody's ever home."

"No one answers the door," I said grouchily.

Shay shrugged. "The check's not worth it to be honest."

"How much?" asked Decker.

"Five," said Shay.

"Dollars?"

"Hundred." I said. "Five hundred. Tight bastards. Most volunteers ask us to redirect the funds back to Charlie's."

I patted my jacket. "I have the check here. Needs a signature. Shit, where's my pen?"

Shay shook his head. Apparently he didn't have one either. "We'll mail the check to you."

"Or we can add it your paycheck?" I offered.

"I have a pen," said Decker.

Shay glanced at his watch and flinched at the time.

"To be honest," said Decker, "I only just started at Charlie's. Haven't seen that first paycheck yet."

"Sorry you didn't get that email."

Decker widened the door. "You can come in if you like."

Shay glanced at me. "I suppose we could get this one done now."

I agreed with a nod.

The house came in around 1000 square feet of chaos. Decker had all the makings of a hoarder, with old pizza boxes strewn here and there, beer cans crushed in the corner, and the only furniture was a well-worn sofa sagging in the middle. The mismatch cushions were stained yellow. The TV was new. Cigarette smoke wafted from a corner ashtray.

"What kind of dog?" said Shay. "Sounds like a poodle. My aunt has a poodle. Smart dogs."

"Rottweiler. Big softy. Unless I'm threatened."

"As it should be," I said.

"How long have you lived here?" asked Shay.

"Just moved in with my brother. Sorry for the mess."

"Your brother doesn't work at Charlie's?" said Shay.

"No, he..." He searched for the answer. "He's got a job."

"Where?" I said casually.

"Who gives a fuck, man," snapped Shay.

He'd seen Decker's left eyelid twitch, hinting at his suspicion. Shay looked annoyed with me. "Give him the check then."

I reached into my pocket.

"Do you have a beer?" said Shay.

"You're not drinking." I removed my hand. "We have ten other stops."

"Just one. Get off my case."

"This always happens." I looked to Decker for support. "He gets drunk and then I have to drive him home to fucking Orange County."

"Drinking is the only way to put up with your bullshit."

I glared at Shay.

"I have to take a piss." Shay rolled his eyes. "Restroom?"

Decker pointed. "Down the hall."

"Which room's your dog in?" asked Shay.

"Bedroom."

"I'm not gonna get my dick ripped off am I?" Shay laughed and headed off.

"Stay out of the bedroom and you'll be fine," Decker shouted after him.

"I'm trying to keep him off the wagon," I muttered.

"You mean on the wagon?"

I scratched my face, as though embarrassed.

He glanced in Shay's direction. "My brother's a drinker. I get it."

"He's into the hard stuff too. I worry about him. He's been there for me. But I'm getting tired of his drug use."

"My brother uses."

"Really?"

"I don't touch the stuff." He raised his hand defensively.

"Tried LSD once," I lied right back. "Acted like I had superhuman powers. Believed I could rip a man's head off with my bare hands." I stared at him then back down at my palms, turning them over as though reminiscing. "Flashbacks are a bitch."

"Bad trip?"

"The worst?" I pointed to the TV. "Nice."

"Yeah."

"Hey," said Shay, appearing from the hallway. "He has a copy of War and Peace in the bathroom."

"Yours?" I asked Decker.

"My brother's."

"I hate reading," said Shay. "Don't see the point."

I arched an amused brow.

Shay was going for a fucking Oscar.

"You're not from around here, are you?" I asked Decker.

"Charlotte."

"What's it like growing up there?"

"Grew up elsewhere."

My movement was slow, deliberate, matching the way he leaned on his left leg, the way he held his hands to his chest defensively, and that tilt of his head.

"I was always in my brother's shadow," I whispered solemnly, matching that lilt in his accent, his tone, cadence.

A subtle mirroring.

"Me too," he muttered.

"Hate to think about it. Bad memories."

"Yeah, well." He narrowed his gaze.

"I blame the way my dad was. Crazy son of a bitch."

"Mine was drunk half the time. The rest of the time he was away at sea."

"Where'd you grow up?"

"Alaska."

"Bet that was fun?"

"If you like wide open spaces."

"Wide open spaces."

"It's kind of lonely, actually."

"Lonely?"

"Ever been?"

"Once."

"I hated it."

"He hit you?" I muttered. "Your dad?"

"Tried to make me a man." He scoffed at that.

"Life hurts," I murmured.

Decker gazed off. "He almost broke my brother's arm once. Shoved him down the stairs. He told my mom Adrian lost his balance."

"How old?"

"17."

"Where was your mom?"

"Around. She was scared of him too."

"Your brother?"

Decker frowned. "I meant my dad."

"Your parents tried to keep you on the straight and narrow," I whispered.

"Suppose."

"They knew."

"Knew?"

"You were both strong willed. Full of possibility. Could have gone either way."

"Yeah, well."

"We blame our parents, but that's a cop out," I said. "There comes a time when we know right from wrong."

He looked at us warily.

"You can either live life well, serve others, be kind and good, or you can choose to be an A-one asshole. Choice is yours ultimately. Apparently you chose the latter."

"What?"

"He called you an asshole," said Shay.

"Why?"

"You're fired," I said flatly.

His jaw gaped.

"We only hire staff with integrity."

"What about my check?"

"There is no check," said Shay.

"I don't understand."

"I'll make it clear," I said. "Tell Adrian I know what he did to Ms. Lauren when she was fourteen. I know he murdered her mother. I have the documented evidence to support this. I also have the D.A.'s involvement. Tell Adrian we have men watching his every move. The statute of limitations may be over for what he did to Mrs. Lauren, but if he so much as steps out of line, I will have him incarcerated for life."

"I didn't do anything."

"You're blackmailing Ms. Lauren. You assaulted her."

"Didn't."

"You ripped off her choker."

"She gave it to me." He glanced toward the bedroom. An unspoken threat he'd let his dog lose.

"I saw the scar you left on her neck."

Though it was nothing compared to the one on her heart.

Decker's face flushed with fury. "Bet Dr. Cole doesn't want the press to find out she's the daughter of a crack addict."

"It's over, Decker," I said calmly.

"Fuck you. Get out."

I stepped closer. "If either of you ever go near Ms. Lauren again, I will eviscerate you."

"That's disembowel," said Shay. "He talks posh."

Decker glanced toward the bedroom again.

"If you attempt to contact her, I will find you and I will end you."

"Who the fuck are you?" he snapped.

"Your worst nightmare."

"Are you…"

"I am." I turned on my heel and left.

Breathing in the cool night air, I was grateful to leave that stench behind. Shay followed me out.

He patted his jacket. "Collar's intact."

"Thank you, Shay. Brilliantly executed."

I hated the thought of them ever touching anything of mine.

"What about the dog?" I said halfway down the pathway, envisioning the animal let loose and taking a bite out of one of us.

"Tranquilizer."

"Ingenious."

"Have my moments." He smiled. "He gobbled up the steak laced with the sedative."

"You really do think of everything."

"Dog protocol." He pulled a face as he tapped his pocket. "My jacket's going to need a dry-clean."

"Throw it away. I'll buy you another."

"I like this one."

"I'll buy you the same one."

"It has sentimental value."

"I'll buy you a boat then."

"You just did."

"Okay, a house."

"Now you're being ridiculous."

We turned the corner.

The SUV, BMW, and Bugatti Veyron were just up ahead. Shay's men looked menacing as they stood guard. They'd attracted the attention of several gangbangers by the look of things, and they lingered not too far away on the street corner, no doubt intrigued by the flashy wheels and flashier entourage.

"That was a big fucking dog," said Shay.

I patted his back in admiration.

"All men accounted for," he said. "Not a bad day."

"Let's find Adrian."

"Well we know where he is now."

"Where?"

"You'll never guess what I found in his bedroom."

My phone buzzed and I snapped it to my ear. "Henry?"

"Where are you?" he said gruffly.

"Are you in the air?"

"Fuck, no. Waiting for you."

I hurried toward the cars. "I'll be there in twenty."

"Good. How's Mia?"

"How did you know?"

"I'm your brother."

"The issue's been resolved."

"Hurry up. I don't know how your evening's going, but mine's grueling."

"In what way?"

"Our air stewardess is a bossy bitch. She has a swastika tattooed on her body somewhere. Ass probably. I'll put money on it."

CHAPTER 4

MIA SLEPT SOUNDLY, but those disheveled sheets indicated remnants of a nightmare. My heart ached for her.

Our luxury 747 had reached cruising altitude several hours ago and we were well on our way to New York. The Cole plane had every luxury—this private bedroom, a conference area, an office, and a small lounge where, right now, Shay and Henry were going over the documents my father's team had emailed us.

His executives were equally immersed, with legal, business, and corporate staff burning the midnight oil to try and salvage our sinking ship.

A break from the intensity was needed and here lay my serenity. I set the ice-filled glass of water down on the night stand.

The minimal décor provided some respite. Those two chairs, the walled TV, and the artwork were all well secured. The deep blue comforter provided the only color.

Very gently, I brushed a stray hair out of Mia's eyes. She stirred awake and blinked up at me.

"How are you feeling?" I said softly.

"Sleepy."

"Keep sleeping. I didn't mean to wake you."

She took in the deepest breath. "What's the time?"

"Midnight."

She rubbed her eyes. "Are you going to get some sleep too?"

"Have some work to do."

"I'm sorry, Cameron."

"What for?" I handed her the glass.

She pushed herself up. "We're on the run again."

I smiled at her. "We're not on the run. And we weren't on the run from Lance. We were merely putting distance between that rogue and us."

She drank. "Why are we going to New York?"

"Business."

"You've relented then?"

"I have."

"What did Adrian say?"

"He wasn't there. Decker was though. He was very compliant."

"You persuaded him?"

"I did."

"Did you give him money?"

"No."

"Good." She blinked at me. "I'm so glad you got the collar back."

"Me too."

"I was terrified they might have sold it."

"That would have been hard."

"Because it's stolen?" She took another sip.

"Yes, and it's worth fifteen million."

She had trouble swallowing. "I would have spanked myself had I known. You could have told me."

"I wanted you to enjoy wearing it."

"Oh, God."

"It's insured."

"Yes, but it belonged to Aunt Rose." She looked pained. "How did you find out about Decker?"

"Staff shared that with Zie. Told her you'd met someone at Charlie's. She told me during her therapy session. I almost believed her."

Mia hugged herself tighter.

My body tensed. "You were seen huddling together."

"We were whispering. I didn't want anyone to overhear what he was saying about me, about my mom. I was embarrassed."

And I'd walked right out of his house without punching him.

My hand balled into a fist instinctively.

"He looked familiar, and when I realized who he was..." she said.

The thought of it had almost destroyed me.

"Why didn't you say something?"

"Same reason you didn't tell me about Decker and Adrian. We were trying to protect each other." I kissed her forehead.

"I thought I could handle them."

"You don't handle these kind of people."

"I really thought if I gave them what they wanted they'd go away. It was only a few thousand at first..."

"Until Decker saw your choker."

She winced.

"It's over," I soothed.

"I'm sorry I lied to you at dinner."

I reached for her hand. "Never lie to me again."

"I promise."

"Mia, I need you to listen. These kind of threats come in every day. That's why we have Shay and his team. They handle all security. If anything ever comes up again, you must tell me. Or Shay, if I'm busy. Straight away. No delay. You never handle any issue alone. Am I understood?"

"I was scared you or your family would suffer because of me."

"Am I understood?" I repeated firmly.

"Yes."

"Mia, I own Chrysalis. Let's be grateful they didn't find that out."

"Could you be connected to it?"

"The ownership goes under a corporation. We call it 'The House' when discussing any details in public. Very ambiguous."

"So it can't be traced back to you?"

Amused, I arched a brow. "That's the benefit of a secret society."

"Thank you for making that go away." She still looked scared.

"It's because of me you were there."

"I'd never forgive myself if my actions hurt you."

I wanted to say, 'Mia, that man murdered your mother. How in God's name could you not have told me? How could you even talk to his brother?'

But I knew the answer. She'd buried her pain to protect me.

"Mia, if anything ever happens to you, it will kill me. Do you hear me? You are the most important part of my world."

She sighed, her face full of worry from those filth drenched hours that still clung to her, threatening never to leave. I wanted to soothe her and remove all anxiety and have her free of the pain that had caught up with her again.

That work I'd done with her in Chrysalis's dungeon had gone a long way to heal her, but the threat had reemerged.

I could see it her eyes.

Those bastards had stirred up a hornet's nest of memories for her, and I refused to allow their effect to linger one more second.

She needed my strength above all things.

I rose from the bed and went over to lock the door. Yes, I was needed out there, but Mia needed me too. As I stripped off my clothes, I vowed I'd give my family every second of every minute of time when I was in New York.

Whatever they asked of me and for however long.

"I don't think you truly comprehend how your happiness affects mine," I said.

"Am I still your submissive?"

"Without question. It's the only way I can keep you out of mischief."

Her eyes widened and she held that caught in the headlights look I adored.

"Cameron, that's a lot of money for a piece of jewelry."

"Not when it comes to you, Mia."

"Your idea of comfortable and mine are two different things."

"I'm not easy to live with. I have unusual needs."

"Like what?" She scraped her teeth over her bottom lip.

"Well, for a start, I demand complete obedience." I took the glass from her and set it down.

She sat up, wrapping the sheet around her, and bowed her head.

"That's a good start. As you know, my submissive must obey me." I tugged back the sheet and exposed her, reaching for her bra and easing it low to reveal both breasts. "She must respond to all orders swiftly." Taking my time, I tweaked her nipples, playing with one and then the other.

I climbed onto the bed and moved back up against the headboard, pulling Mia toward me. She straddled my lap and faced me.

"You need a cuddle," I whispered, and buried my head into her nape, breathing her in.

"I love you," she whispered.

I pulled her away from me. "I told you I'd protect you."

"How did you find me?"

"Your love was a beacon."

She thumped my arm.

I laughed and reached for my jacket and pulled out that envelope I'd stuffed in there before leaving home. I slid out the contract and unfolded it. Arching a curious brow, I reviewed her signature.

Then I saw the number. "You amended the document on the hard drive?"

"Might have."

She'd taken off the last two zeros of the amount offered in the NDA agreement, lessening the settlement to 2,500 dollars. A small token should we not work out, and the legalese to protect me from a 'tell-all' down the line.

Though Mia would never do that to me. I knew this with certainty. It was Dominic, my lawyer, who insisted on it.

Mia peeked down at the form. "I'll only need a few thousand for a deposit on an apartment. If we don't work out."

"Don't say it like that."

"Well that's what's it's for, right?" She shrugged. "I've always been independent. That's never going to change."

"I warned you of the consequences."

"Something about punishing me with your—" She wiggled her eyebrows.

"No, I distinctly remember telling you there'd be no further access to my most valuable asset."

"Should have been clearer."

"You took a risk."

"Goes both ways, Cameron. If you want a pass to my pussy, you're going to have to—"

I kissed her hard. A fierce fucking of her mouth with my tongue that silenced her rebellion.

"Remove your panties."

She slipped them off, her gaze moving from me then back to her nakedness. Her vulnerability was glaring.

With my hands on her hips, I directed her sex along my cock, and she trembled with pleasure as her clit stroked back and forward along my full length.

"Enjoying that?" I asked huskily.

"Yes." Her lips parted and her eyelids lowered.

"I'm a man of my word, Mia."

She titled her head back slightly to better look at me.

The hum of the plane's engine and the warmth in here lulled us.

I gripped her hips and lifted her so she stood on the bed looking down at me.

"I'm merciful at least." I kissed her sex.

She leaned against me, pressing both palms on the curved wall for balance.

I devoured her, suckling, swirling my tongue over her, and her thighs trembled, her breathing grew ragged. I imagined she was silently begging me not to cease my flicking and I gave in to her need, ignoring my own. Flicking faster, now and again I stopped so I could gently nip her clit. Then I let go, allowing that delicate nub to engorge and bring a wave of pleasure. Her soft moans willed me on. Mia rocked her hips, caressing herself over my tongue. Her shuddering was endless as she came hard, with a long moan stifled as she bit down on her hand.

She lowered herself and sat on my lap and reached for my groin.

I grabbed her wrist and pulled it away. "As soon as you sign the original document."

"You're not serious?"

"I am."

"But Cameron?"

I kissed her nose. "You'll cave."

To show she was up for the challenge, she arched her brows defiantly.

"We'll see, Madam," I said.

She twisted her mouth thoughtfully.

"Mia, never again keep anything from me. Understand?"

"Yes."

I cupped her face with both hands and stared into her eyes. "I demand honesty from you. It's the only way I can protect you."

"I'll never let you down again."

"It's not because I'm some egotistical bastard who likes to keep track of his lover to the point of obsession. It's because of the family I was born into."

Her pupils remained dilated. Those soft blue irises were easy to fall into.

"My family is rich and powerful. What you don't know, or could never know, is what this truly means."

She reached out and grasped my forearms.

"Mia, we're talking the kind of money that brings great power. Friends are actually your enemies."

"Why do it then?"

"We bring tea to the masses. The company has grown into a global brand. With that comes unprecedented power. The benefits include bigger homes, faster boats, private jets, and enough champagne to drown in. The grandest prize of course is the prestige. The political power one has access to. The ability to influence world affairs."

"Your father?"

"His first born was Cole Tea and we are constantly reminded of the fact."

"I know he loves you."

"Perhaps now you understand why I wanted no part in it other than the charities?"

"You prefer medicine."

"There's plenty of good the business does, and its charities have thrived because of my parents philanthropic pursuits."

"You never considered going into the business?"

"It's a life I've avoided." I let out a long sigh of regret. "Yes, there's the power I lord over Enthrall and Chrysalis, but that's nothing compared to what it would be like to run Cole Tea. I love my life. I love you at the center of it.'

Mia was my light. My oxygen. The very air I breathed.

I pressed a fingertip to her lips. "I ask for honesty. I owe you the same privilege."

Her frown deepened.

"The reason we're flying to New York is serious."

"Oh?"

"There's an unprecedented attack on my family's business. It's what's known as a hostile takeover."

"What does it mean?"

"An acquisition company has gone directly to the shareholders in an endeavor to remove my father's hold on Cole Tea. A tender offer was placed to merge with another company. We rejected it. We're under attack from a proxy fight. If there's a simple majority vote agreeing within the shareholders to replace the management, the takeover will happen. The shareholders listen to the board. The board is moving forward with the takeover."

Mia cringed. "Oh no, you were running all over L.A. looking for me."

"A slight detour."

"There must be something your family can do?"

There was a knock at the door.

"Yes?" I said.

"Dr. Cole," came the Irish lilt of Irene, our overly formal stewardess. "Your presence has been requested, sir."

"Tell them I'll be right there." I hoped Shay and Henry had found something of use.

"Yes, sir." Irene's footsteps fell away.

"Cameron," whispered Mia. "What can I do?"

"Be you."

"I'll make you proud."

"You already do."

"It's going to be rough, isn't it?"

"It's going to be bloody."

"We've faced worst monsters, Cameron."

I stared into her eyes.

"The ones inside our mind can do just as much damage," she whispered. "If we let them."

"True."

"I believe in you. If anyone can save Cole Tea, it's you."

"With you by my side."

She reached for my cock and I slapped her hand away.

She gasped in surprise.

I grinned as I studied Mia's soulful expression and I reached

25

around to the back of her head to grab a handful of locks. Shifting my hips, positioning my cock at her entrance, I then slid all the way in, enveloping myself in the snugness of her sex.

Her breath stuttered. "Cameron."

I pulled her toward me and whispered, "Forget the contract. We're never going to need it."

CHAPTER 5

LAUGHTER CARRIED UP the aisle of the plane.

Shay and Henry were sharing a joke and laughing hysterically, their legs stretched out on their footrests. Both of them were covered in a tartan blanket.

"I was told you wanted to see me?" I frowned at them playfully.

Shay beamed. "We've been tucked in."

My gaze followed his toward the cockpit and settled on Irene, our redheaded stewardess. She seemed busy with the post take off checks.

Two hours ago she'd welcomed me, Shay, and Mia aboard the flight with a big Irish smile and the confidence to match. Her hair was up in a neat chignon and her stewardess uniform showed off her curves and provided an air of professionalism. Her makeup was flawless and made her look younger than her early thirties. Those deep green eyes fixed on our every move until we'd secured our seatbelts.

Irene had disappeared inside the galley, giving us all a moment to catch our breath after the day we still hadn't quite caught up with, and for us to steady our nerves after that turbulent takeoff. I agreed with Henry. Irene hid her bad girl tattoo somewhere and something told me Henry would find out exactly where later.

"She scares the shit out of me," he said with a smirk.

This sent Shay into another round of laughter.

I fell into the big seat next to Shay's, laughing just as hard. It was great to see Henry relaxed considering the circumstances of why we were on this flight.

"We were making too much noise," said Henry.

"She told you that?" I said.

"Irene asked us to be a little quieter," explained Shay.

"She was concerned you and Mia were sleeping." Henry arched a brow.

"Mia's asleep now," I said. "Coffee?"

We ordered drinks and Shay and Henry righted their chairs and pulled their blankets off them.

Shay had already filled Henry in on the Herron brothers and our final hours in L.A. Watching Henry's reaction made me realize Decker was lucky he'd had to deal with me and not Henry. Decker would have been hospitalized had Henry met him.

"We're handling them," I told him.

Shay leaned forward and rested his elbows on his knees. "Adrian's working as a security guard. His spare uniform was on a hanger."

"Do we know where?"

"His ID gave it away. Burbank Mall."

"We have him."

"How did he get a job working there?" asked Henry.

"He's a criminal without a record."

Shay confirmed with a nod. "A DUI in Charlotte, fifteen years ago. That's it."

"Still drug dealing?" I asked.

"We'll know soon," said Shay. "I'll have them tracked."

"Fill me in on any developments. Let's keep Mia out of this for now."

"Sure."

We moved into the conference section and took advantage of the table surrounded by six fixed chairs then readied ourselves for the long night ahead. Henry opened his laptop and we sat around with a clear view of the screen. He brought up the list of names for all ten board members.

"Here's what we know so far," he said. "Two weeks ago the board members were each approached and offered some kind of deal."

"We have a spy?" I said.

"Not a member of the board," said Henry. "Javier Marcotte is Dad's old executive assistant and now works for Jeff Livingston, one of the board members. Javier still keeps Dad updated on the rumor mill."

"Impressive," said Shay.

"Dangerous for Javier," I said. "But necessary."

Irene pushed her cart down the aisle and prepped the coffee.

"That better be Tempest," said Henry dryly.

"Of course, sir," she said. "We only have Cole Tea and Tempest Coffee on this flight."

"Glad to hear it."

"Thank you for hosting our flight," I said. "I know it's late, and this was last minute."

"I'm on call," she said. "Your dad's assistant told me this was important." She looked over at Henry. "I'm sorry about earlier. Your father insisted we took off as soon as possible."

"We needed Dr. Cole on board too." Henry gestured to me. "Sorry I made your job more difficult, Irene. That wasn't my intention."

Her face softened and her blush rose. "No need to apologize, sir."

"Henry's a war vet," Shay told her.

"I read that about you," she said, looking over at him.

Henry winced.

"Which article was it?" I took the mug from Irene. "Thank you."

"The one in the L.A. times. Mr. Cole senior gave me it to read during a flight from India a few years back." She handed Henry his coffee. "Your dad's so proud of you."

Henry looked over at me.

"He's the bravest man I know," I said warmly. "Hell, he's the most incredible man I know."

Shay pointed at Henry. "We served in Afghanistan together. This officer put himself in danger to save his men. That's the kind of man he is."

"I'm not running for office," said Henry. "So you can pull back on the elaboration."

Shay leaned forward. "Henry, you knew men would die unless you entered that town to get them."

"They were rescued because of you," I said.

"And we all know what my reward was," said Henry.

"A Purple Heart?" said Irene brightly.

Henry stared at her blankly. "That's in a box now. Somewhere."

"Did my father ever mention me?" I tried to change the subject.

"I'm sorry," Irene stuttered. "I didn't mean—"

"I rarely discuss it," said Henry. "Forgive me."

"I should get back." She glanced toward the front of the plane.

"Some milk perhaps?" I said warmly.

She poured milk into my mug. "You're a doctor?"

I ignored my brother's knowing stare.

She added milk into their coffees too. "Dr. Cole, is it true you once finished the New York Times crossword puzzle in under four minutes?"

"Don't remember that," I said.

"You're dad told me he'd only put the paper down for a few minutes and when he picked it up again you'd finished it."

"So nothing about my work then?"

Irene looked surprised. "You were nine."

"Years old?" asked Shay.

"Yes," she said. "Apparently."

I shrugged. "So no mention of my work?"

"We don't really talk that much. Sorry. Your dad works during each flight. He never sleeps. Never watches a movie. Makes calls. Works on his laptop."

"This is great coffee," I said.

"Of course it is." Irene smiled, then she pushed her cart off up the aisle.

"She didn't offer us peanuts," said Henry.

"Nine years old," said Shay. "Seriously, Cameron, how did you do that?"

"Must have known the answers."

Shay leaned forward on his elbows. "When did you first realize you were smarter than everyone else?"

"Wouldn't say that."

"Then how would you say it?"

"Maybe it's because of nut allergies," Henry said.

Shay chuckled. "Bet you know the answer to that one too, Cam."

I pushed myself to my feet. "I'll get some."

"How do you know she has any?" said Shay, impressed. "Residual salt on Irene's fingertips from where she's eaten a packet herself. An empty packet in the trash?"

I beamed at him. "They were on the cart."

More laughter flowed.

Having calmed a devastated Irene over forgetting to deliver our snacks, I returned to my seat and was rewarded with cheers. I handed over the chips, peanuts, and chocolate covered pretzels. "We've been warned not to ruin our appetites. Irene's bringing menus."

"Dinner or breakfast?" asked Shay.

"Whatever you like."

"So glad you got a taste of her bossiness," said Henry.

I glanced back to make sure she didn't hear. "Actually, Henry, she's rather compliant."

"What did you say to her?"

"I told her we valued her time."

"And?" said Shay.

The look I gave Shay told him Irene leaned toward submission.

"Perfect," said Shay. "With your permission, I'd like to set up a date?"

"I thought you had a girlfriend?" said Henry.

"Not for me."

"In that case." Henry rose to his feet. "I don't mind if I do." He headed up the aisle.

"Well," I said. "Looks like he's going to discover Irene's tattoo."

Within a few minutes, Henry returned.

"That was quick," said Shay.

"Got her phone number," said Henry, sitting back down. "You didn't' seriously think I was going to…"

Shay shook his head.

I held back on a grin, avoiding eye contact with them.

Henry blew a cold stream of air on his drink. "You guys are incorrigible."

We spent the flight drowning in even more coffee to stay awake while scrolling through Dad's emails that had gone back and forth between the main office and the board members, hoping to get a feel on their ability to be swayed.

Mia joined us after taking an hour long nap. We set about reviewing the social media sites, reading communications related to Cole Tea, and looking for any suspicious negative marketing campaigns that might have rendered the business vulnerable.

"Nothing," said Henry. "There's nothing anywhere."

Shay held my gaze. "They've done this before."

CHAPTER 6

IN THE HEART of Manhattan, nestled in the Upper East Side, rested one of New York's biggest mansions.

The surrounding buildings belong to numerous museums and schools and a few other homes owned by the ultra-rich. This imperial structure honored the once popular Georgian vision, with its spectacular façade, and was once the home of my childhood.

Henry, Shay, Mia, and I stood in the foyer.

The butler had gone off to let my mother know we'd arrived.

All of us lined up shoulder to shoulder, and we were equally intimidated by all this splendor.

This place was vast.

Early morning sunlight burst into the foyer—an assault on both my eyes and the rest of my senses. I'd still not slept, though was reassured Shay, Henry, and Mia had gotten some sleep during the flight.

The décor was decadently layered in burgundy drapes, giant vases, dramatic ten foot paintings, and gold plated everything. The designer had seemingly picked up France's Palace of Versailles and set it down here.

Over there, in the left hand corner, I'd broken my big toe as a kid when I'd run into that Qing Dynasty vase and it had tipped over and landed on my foot. The vase was fine apparently, and Nanny had kept her promise to never report the mishap to Mom.

Henry and I had run up and down those stairs so many times

as cowboys, soldiers, and alien invaders, sweeping down the banister with alarming speed and keeping the staff busy with our boundless energy.

I was glad Henry was here now.

"They've redone the place," his whisper echoed.

"How many bedrooms?" said Shay.

"Can't remember," I said.

"That's a big house then."

I nudged Mia's arm. "We have a pool."

"Is the water piped in from somewhere exclusive?" she said.

"Don't be ridiculous," said Henry. "Everyone knows the pool is filled with unicorn tears."

Mia giggled.

"Not bad for New York," said Shay. "Not bad at all."

"Richard should be here," I whispered.

Shay gave a nod. "Your parents love Richard. We'd have gotten a pass if he'd been with us."

"Here you are!" It was Willow, and she hurried across the marble floor barefoot, wearing a flowing white dress. She was the breath of fresh air we all needed.

Willow fell into my arms and I hugged her. "Good to see you, Will."

"I'm so glad you're here." She ran over to Henry and hugged him too, moving on to hug Shay and then Mia. She came back to me and took my hand. "Mother's not doing well. The stress of it all has been too much for her. Father's in the study."

"How's he doing?" I said.

"In denial."

"We're here now. We'll turn this around."

"I'm afraid there's not much to be done," she said. "The board visited this morning. They had brunch with Daddy and delivered the news they've made up their minds and, well, that's that."

"Dad's not going to fight them?" asked Henry.

"There's nothing to fight. Monday morning they'll present their vote."

"There's still time," I said.

"I'll go check on Mom," said Henry.

"Willow, do you mind showing Shay and Mia to their rooms?" I said.

"Sure."

"Where's Dad?"

"Study." She looked sheepish. "I'm afraid Mom's a little old fashioned."

"Mom has Mia and I in separate rooms?"

She bit her lip apologetically.

"That's fine," I said, marveling how two sisters could be so different, with Aunt Rose so open minded and Mom prudish. "See that they're adjoining."

"That I can do. Come on, Mia, let's catch up. I'm so happy you're here. Cameron tells me you're a strong swimmer. We have a pool."

Mia flashed Henry a smile then gave a subtle gesture of support to me with her clenched fist.

Henry, Mia, and Shay headed up the central staircase behind Willow.

Shay threw me an expression of utter awe.

I headed off toward the study.

CHAPTER 7

DAD SAT AT his desk with his focus on a small marble plate set before him.

Lifting a few loose tea leaves between his thumb and forefinger, he brought them to his nose to sniff. He was lost in thought.

His office was full of antiques. That writing desk over there had been crafted in India over a hundred years ago. Those book cases had been shipped in from England and could boast an impressive collection of books written by famous poets, collected from his extensive travels.

He could point to that enormous globe on a stand and boast he'd visited most of the countries on there. Though not jungles. He hated snakes, so dense vegetation was strictly avoided.

Dad wasn't just a formidable business man, he was also a craftsman. I'd often watched him blend teas. As a seasoned teaologist, he created masterpieces that went on to become bestsellers around the world. It was relaxing to watch him work methodically, creating blends and boosting the complexity of flavor, aroma, and taste.

As a teenager he'd been taught the ancient art of the tea ceremony, just as his father had been, and his before him. An extraordinary legacy.

And despite my reluctance towards the business, there'd always been a pride in who we were and what my father had achieved.

"Hey Dad," I said softly and sat in the chair opposite his desk.

"Cameron?" He roused from his daze. "So glad you came."

"Henry's gone up to check on Mom."

He brushed tea leaves off his fingers. "How was your flight?"

The formality hurt worse than it should.

"Pleasant."

Turbulent.

"It's been quite the experience," he said. "Lots of activity in the house. Your mom will be pleased you're here."

"How are you holding up?"

"Not bad, considering." He nudged the marble plate toward me. "Sniff."

I leaned in, closed my eyes, and breathed in the aroma. "A long walk in the city. Pine trees, fresh cut grass—" I breathed in another whiff— "Christmas in New York."

"Good job."

"Perhaps I can take some home?"

"You're not staying?"

"I didn't mean…of course, for as long as I'm needed."

"The issue's been resolved. Not an ideal outcome. Swift but sure."

I sat back, stunned.

I'd always resisted the idea my father and I were alike, fearing I too could be as cold.

He pointed to the plate. "Baked over charcoal. Leaves from India."

"And blended by you."

He gave a shrug. "Maybe I'll move to Kentucky and buy a racecourse. Willow would like that."

"Mom might be a little vexed."

"She'll get over her fall from grace when she realizes what kind of real estate we can get for the same price of this house."

"It will be sad to sell this place."

"So many memories."

Fewer for me after a childhood spent at boarding school.

He shook his head. "We have the photos."

I doubted there were any of me. I took another sniff of tea, suppressing this discomfort.

Dad stared at me. "I wanted you well out of the way."

"Excuse me?"

"Growing up. As a boy."

"Understandable," I said, my voice surprisingly strong.

"Didn't want you anywhere near those thugs."

My gaze rose from the tea to meet his.

"When I took over from your grandfather, there was still the residual mafia bullies. Many businesses in New York were subject to the stranglehold of the La Cosa Nostra."

"Crime families?"

"Gambino, Colombo, Luchese, Bonanno, and Genovese maintained order with a strict hierarchy. Their rule was so fierce the very profits they sought could just as easily dissipate when the businesses they crippled went under." Dad brought the plate back to his side. "Today we merely hand it over to legal."

My father's legal team Blander, Fleiss, and Remington was the very best money could buy.

"Back then, when you were a boy, they went after the family," he said. "It was best to tuck you away safely where no one could reach you."

Not even my parents apparently, with rare visits and rarer trips home. Which left little sentimentality for this place and its overreaching social splendor.

"You should have explained this to us," I said.

"And scare you? Heavens no."

"I'm glad you're sharing it with me now."

He looked surprised. "You were always so defiant."

Those tea leaves took on a shape, their scattered edges forming fragility.

"I'm addicted to Cole's Coconut Tea." I tried to lift the tension.

"You always did have a sweet tooth." He frowned. "You were nine when I first realized."

"Realized?"

"How damn smart you are. We played chess for the first time that Christmas. We were snowed in." He looked over at the fireplace. "Right over there. Do you remember?"

"Yes."

"You won, Cameron."

"You let me."

"Didn't."

I arched a brow. "I was excited to spend time with you. I wanted to impress you."

"Told your mother that Cole Tea was going to be in good hands. What with your brother's bravery and your brilliance."

"And Willow?"

"Prefers horses."

"All grown up."

"I remember finding a stash of dolls under your bed once," he said. "I was so worried about you. Really believed you were showing signs of…"

"Homosexuality?"

He waved it off. "Turned out your sister was going through a phase of pulling the arms and legs off her dolls. You were—"

"Trying to save them." I chuckled at the memory of me gathering them up and hoping not to get caught.

"Blonde Barbies, I think." He thinned his lips. "Thank goodness she's over that."

"Willow was six, Dad." I shook my head. "Exploring her world through toys."

"We were worried for a while there."

"She only did it once."

"Because you hid the rest." He smiled. "You never dated blondes. Always brunettes. Probably traumatized by your sister."

"Mia's blonde."

"Is she here?"

"Yes."

He arched an amused brow. "Perhaps this means you've finally recovered from your childhood trauma." Dad sighed deeply. "When I snapped that bird's neck, I knew you were watching."

He'd put that dying bird out of its misery. Ten minutes before I'd found it in the garden and brought it to him, hoping he could save it.

"A healthy introduction to death," I said sarcastically.

"You were too soft."

"I was five."

He looked surprised.

"You're lucky I'm not a sociopath."

He scoffed. "Like your father."

"Funny. You're a good man. Dedicated to the business. You've made it one of the leading corporations in the world. It's worth fighting for."

"I'm ready to retire."

"I know."

"I was fighting for every Cole who came before me and the ones who I hoped would follow." His gaze held mine.

"There's still time."

"They won't relent, Cam. They've made up their minds."

"What do you think influenced their decision?"

"Profit margins I suppose."

"Henry and I didn't come all this way to do nothing. We're going to fight to the end, Dad."

"Three moves, Cameron."

"Sorry?"

"You won that chess game in three moves."

"Luck."

"No, you were three moves ahead." He narrowed his gaze. "You're always ahead of everyone. That's probably why we clash."

"A healthy disagreement now and again."

"Your brother was meant to take over, but you were the one who always showed an aptitude. I know you love your profession, but they're not so unlike each other. Both of them require dedication." He raised his stare and held mine. "Mindfulness."

"You have my undivided attention."

He shifted a thick file across the desk and flipped it open. "Take a look."

The names of the board members were listed in alphabetical order on the front page.

"You speed read?" he said.

"This is the contract for the board?"

"Perhaps you'll find something."

I flipped through and caught the number on the last page. "This is five hundred pages. Perhaps have your attorney who wrote it go over it with you?"

"He's dead."

"What?"

"Dan Stork suffered a heart attack on the golf course."

"When?"

"Three weeks ago."

"I'm sorry to hear that."

A headache loomed.

"Dan inserted some ambiguous wording into the contract. Tucked it away in there to protect me should I ever need it."

"He didn't tell you where?"

"Died the morning before our meeting."

I stared at the file. "You want me to find some vague wordage?"

"Pretty much."

"You should hand this over to your lawyers."

"They're focused on salvaging what they can."

"Dad?" I sat back. "What aren't you telling me?"

"Our current threat is linked to someone in legal."

"And you know this how?"

"There's evidence. We tracked the IP address to the legal department."

"And?"

"The account was deleted. IT hit a dead end."

"Fire everyone. Hire a new team."

"There's no time."

"This is not what I do, Dad."

He reached for the file to take it back.

I pulled it toward me, my mind spiraling. "Cole Tea is important to me. We're not going down without a fight."

He gave a wry grin. "Perhaps you're my Trojan horse, Cam."

CHAPTER 8

THE LAUNDRY ROOM felt cozy.

I sat with my back against the Whirlpool washing machine, stealing a moment of privacy, needing time to think.

I was running on adrenaline and caffeine and couldn't remember what sleep felt like. Nausea welled.

"You're not staying," I told myself, as though laying down a lifeline at my feet, ready for when I chose to bail.

Now felt like a good time.

That five hundred page document waited for me in my assigned bedroom. The mission threatened to eat up my time. My childhood bedroom had long ago been demolished in a remodeling, though there was comfort in knowing that room no longer existed.

I regretted agreeing to Dad's impossible task. There was no time to bury my head in legalese looking for the proverbial needle in a haystack. And there was no way to be sure I'd know what it was when I found it.

I was going to be dealing with the best minds in business— men and women who'd dedicated their lives to the study of capitalism.

On the flight over, I'd explained to Mia the kind of people we were up against. I'd been psyching myself up too, I realized that now, persuading myself I had what it took to face the cutthroats that surrounded our business like sharks circling their prey.

Sharks can't swim backwards, I mused. There had to be some

wisdom in there somewhere. Richard loved sharks. Always had.

I pulled out my phone and searched for his number.

The heat from the dryers held in here and kept the chill of winter at bay. This big old house never kept its warmth. Over in that very corner, I'd played with toy soldiers I'd borrowed from Henry. He'd already been shipped off to boarding school. I'd run from room to room and not see anyone for hours. A child left to his own devices, but reasonably safe, locked away in this bastion of Cole power.

How quickly melancholy crept up.

I pressed my phone against my ear.

"I heard you're bailing on my party?" Richard said on the other end.

"I'm sorry."

"I left you a message at your office to call me. Thought you'd lost your phone."

"I'm in New York."

"Manhattan?"

"Yes."

"I wanted to give you the heads up about your Cole Teas shares. Though I'm assuming your dad might have mentioned it by now."

"Richard." His name came out in a rush.

"Hey, are you okay?"

"Hostile takeover. Hasn't hit the press."

"Fuck."

Swallowing hard, I tried to find the words.

"Talk to me."

"I'm here to salvage."

"How's your dad?"

"Not good."

Silence lingered on the other end.

"You don't have too much invested in Cole shares compared to the other stock, so you're solid financially."

"Why is that?"

"I manage your shares."

The correct response was lost on me.

"Can I do anything?"

"You've always loved sharks, Richard. I never asked why?"

"You did ask me once, during a session."

"That's right."

"I told you to fuck off and stop asking me questions."

"I remember."

"Hadn't talked for weeks. You cracked me open like a nut. Used a psychological sledgehammer on me. Now you can't get me to shut up." He sighed deeply. "Sharks keep the ecosystem in balance."

"You're searching for balance."

"I suppose we all are. You know me. If it's frightening, I have to find out why. Sharks are not unlike humans in that if you show you're not intimidated they'll leave you alone. Stare them off. Bully them back and they relent." He laughed.

"What's so funny?"

"You were feared at Harvard. You intimidated everyone with your intellect. The girls were too scared to approach you and the men weren't quite sure how to take you."

"I was friendly."

"Your quick wit could decimate an ego," he said. "When we first met, I was immediately intrigued."

"Are you saying I'm like a shark?"

"You're misunderstood."

"You always got me."

"Same here. Want me to fly out there?"

"I've got this, Richard. This feels like self-fulfilling prophecy."

"Get your shark fin on."

Swim backwards…

"Prepare to freefall," he said.

I let out a slow, steady breath.

"Cameron," he said quietly. "Sharks can see in the dark."

CHAPTER 9

HENRY PULLED THE door closed to Mom's bedroom.

I strolled toward him along the sprawling corridor inlaid with white marble. Upon the walls hung large, High Renaissance paintings—all dramatic religious images that would have been just at home in the Vatican, and none of them conducive to calming the soul. Mom had told me she'd purchased them while visiting family in Rome.

Apparently Raphael's young assistant had masterfully mimicked his work and these were proof of that. These dramatic styles had influenced the Renaissance and Baroque periods and changed the landscape of art irrevocably.

Henry tucked his hands into his pockets and paused before the painting depicting George and the Dragon. The horse glanced back lovingly at his rider as a knighted George pierced a spear through the dragon's heart.

Henry pointed to it. "He practiced on this one. The final version's hanging in the National Gallery in Washington."

"Raphael's assistant?"

Henry smiled. "Mom told you that so you wouldn't be on her case."

My gaze shot to the painting. "Everyone lies."

"Except you, Cam."

My gaze took in the painting, stunned that the hand of Raphael had touched the artwork and disconcerted it was merely hanging in a New York residence.

I made a mental note to discuss their security system with them.

I pointed to Mom's bedroom. "How is she?"

"Taking a nap before lunch."

"Should I go in?"

"She'll be up soon." He looked over at the dragon and arched a brow.

He made me chuckle. "How are you?"

"Good. Let's freshen up and regroup after lunch."

"Good idea."

He gestured behind me and I turned to see Shay. "Hey there."

"Lunch is at one," Henry told us.

"I'll be there," I said.

Henry ambled off.

Shay neared me, his gaze sweeping over the painting. "Can we talk?"

"Sure. Let's go to your room. How is it?"

He shook his head solemnly. "I'm tempted to sleep on the floor."

We headed off down the hallway and we rounded the corner.

Shay opened the door and I followed him in.

We both took a moment to absorb the grandeur. Shay wouldn't know that several of those paintings were by Van Dyck, or that the sculpture in the corner was by Canova. He would however be awestruck by the grand four-poster-bed, the comforter made with gold braid, the material woven in Italy.

"It's just a bed sheet," I said, amused.

"It's like going back in time." He pointed to the chairs and their gold braided fabric. "How's your dad?"

"Holding up."

"What're his thoughts on the future?"

"He's trying to come to terms with it. The betrayal of the board hurts like hell. He's put their kids through school, visited the members when in hospital, paid off their debts, and ensured their grandchildren's future."

Shay blinked at me. "Can't believe it."

"As they say, the nature of business is business."

"It's cutthroat."

I blew out a long sigh. "I will wallow in the blood of my enemies and see no man is left in doubt of my power."

"Who said that?" Shay flinched. "Your dad?"

"Overheard him when I was home from boarding school one evening. Someone had crossed him."

"Was he ever like that with you?" He stared at me for the longest time. "Is that why you're into pain?"

"Analyzing me?"

He broke my gaze. "Impressive house."

"But not a home."

"What was it like growing up here?"

"Cold."

And cold.

I shook off this veil of melancholy and patted Shay on the back. "I'm glad you're here."

"Cam, I'm going to head back to L.A. My replacement will be here soon."

My gut twisted and I tried to read his expression for why.

"Let me explain," he said. "My lack of focus put Mia in danger. You need someone who's not…"

"Not?"

"Distracted."

"Because we're good friends?"

He broke my gaze and walked over to the fireplace, staring into the large mirror above it.

"Shay, talk to me."

"I've crossed the line."

I neared him. "Our lifestyle is who we are—"

"It's complicated."

"My specialty."

"Do you remember that night in the Duoppioni Room? Back at Chrysalis? It was the evening you officially gave me Arianna."

"I remember."

"It was you, me, Arianna—"

"And Ryan Dolton."

The dom who'd trained her.

Shay shook his head. "My first time taking on a sub and I was so damn excited. My heart was bursting out of my chest. I'd only been a member of Chrysalis for a month."

"You did great."

He turned away to hide that soft blush.

That late night scene had been meticulously crafted...

The lighting dimmed, the music soft and alluring...

Ryan, Arianna's dom, had admirably prepared her. With years of experience as a submissive, Arianna had needed little preparation. Though she still challenged any master, and I knew she'd be a great first submissive for Shay.

He'd asked me to be with him that evening. See it through with him. I'd honored his request for there to be no audience.

Arianna had been tied down to the central table in that grand dungeon, a ball gag in her mouth to prevent her cursing. She loved using expletives, which always got her into more trouble. More punishments had to be dished out.

That evening was no exception. Legs splayed, her pussy flinched in readiness. Her thighs were soaking wet from her dom playing with and teasing her sex for the last hour. She'd been disobedient, and her punishment was endless clit play with no relief.

Arianna's toned, naked form was exquisitely inked. A living, breathing unique piece of art. Her bellybutton and clit piercings caught the light.

She'd shuddered in pleasure when Shay had caressed her calves lovingly. His hands shook subtly as he explored her clit ring.

The time had arrived for him to take his place as her new master.

He'd stood between her thighs, his poetic words spoken to her as he promised his commitment. The master's pledge to protect, love, and serve. His deep, booming voice lulled her into submission and she'd gazed at Shay, yearning to be fucked by him.

Ryan Dolton had willingly handed her over. His work was done. His goodbye to her was him coming over her breasts and, much to Arianna's delight, Ryan rubbed his cum into her nipples, sending her into a writing bliss.

"I couldn't get my condom on I was shaking so badly," whispered Shay, proving he too was back in that moment.

Stepping up that day, I'd naturally assisted Shay by taking the condom packet from him, ripping it open, and pinching the end of the rubber before slipping it over the full length of him, grasping firmly as I rolled it down his impressive cock. He'd stiffened further beneath my grip and gave a soft moan of pleasure.

Gripping him for perhaps a few seconds longer than I should have to calm him.

And it had.

On my nod of approval, he'd stepped up, his erection sliding into Arianna's pussy all the way. His slow steady fucking drew out the ritual and solidified its meaning.

She'd bucked as she came. He'd yelled out his orgasm and, afterward, he'd been a changed man. Or so he'd told me during those long hours we'd continued his training as a dom. He'd shown reluctance to cease playing with his new sub.

Shay gave a nod, as though confirming his point was being made even though no words were being spoken.

"When I fucked her," he said wistfully, "I had my eyes closed because part of me wanted it to be you."

"I know."

He looked over at me. "I'm thrown." He made a gesture. "It's not all this. It's…"

I neared him and rested a fingertip beneath his chin, tipping it up, looking deep into his eyes. "Will you do something for me?"

"Anything."

"Go take a shower and jerk off nice and slow. Come hard. Then take a dip in the pool and swim off all this tension. We've been pushed to the limit the last twenty-four hours. We're having lunch in an hour. I want you there."

He looked defeated. "I don't have anything to wear."

"Check the wardrobe. Penny ensured we'd all have what we needed upon our arrival."

His gaze shot to the wardrobe. "For me too?"

"For everyone."

"When?"

"I made the call from the plane. She made it happen. It's what Penny does. You know that."

"You'll never want to fence with me again."

"On the contrary. It's what we both need. As soon as we get back to L.A. we'll fence."

"Cameron, my feelings for you—"

49

"Cancel your replacement. This is not the time for strangers."

"What if this puts you at risk?"

"You've been nothing but professional."

"Until now."

"I value honesty."

"I just have to face you again."

"Shay, you faced off with a Rottweiler for me."

"Exactly. I'm thinking with my balls, Cam."

"Your submissive side's rising to the surface, Shay. I take full responsibility. You and I both know you're a switch. I'm going to find you a male dominant to satisfy you."

"I always fight it."

"As expected. A challenge any worthy dom revels in."

"You need—"

"You focused. Your expertise is essential. Promise me your best."

"Dr. Cole, you have it.'

"Shay, your passion is the loyalty I need." I gave a warm smile.

And left the room.

CHAPTER 10

CARRYING THAT MAMMOTH document with me, I went in search of Mia.

My suspicion of which room Mom might have placed her in was right. The smallest of all the guest bedrooms. Mia knelt on a chair facing the window, ear buds in, listening to music. Her gaze focused on the garden.

She hadn't heard me enter so I took advantage of enjoying watching her.

I placed the file on the bedside table.

The décor leaned toward a country theme and I wondered why this one had been chosen for her. Deep green draped window frames, a soft Persian carpet, damask wallpaper, and that Sèvres porcelain vase standing alone on a long thin shelf.

And then I saw it, hanging on the far wall.

Monachine in Riva Al Mare—the painting by Vincenzo Cabiance— 'Little Nuns by the Sea.' A group of sisters from St. Vincent de' Paoli, standing and chatting with each other on a hill overlooking the ocean.

This house and these preordained rules of who was welcome and who wasn't. A class system with its formulated prejudices had no place in the world I'd created around me.

I no longer belonged here. Never had. Not really.

Mia turned and smiled back at me. The sunlight caught in wisps of her hair. Her smile let me in and locked out the world. As it always did.

She was my peace, my serenity, and I needed her now more than ever. Mia would always represent innocence to me. She'd always be just as pure as those Italian nuns on that hill. But Mia would know the love of a man, feel his arms around her, receive his tender kisses and, not unlike God, I'd protect her until my dying day.

Mia had slipped into my life with the ease of a sacred miracle.

I made my way in and stood at the center and stared at her. From her expression, I could see she was trying to read mine.

"Submissive," I whispered.

She came toward me and knelt at my feet, her head bowed, her gaze lowered, her palms turned up on her thighs, knowing what I needed was this.

"Mia," I said. "I'm going to have to fuck you very hard."

I gestured for her to rise.

With a sweep of my hand, I gave my next command.

She dragged her dress up and over her head and quickly removed her panties and bra, standing naked before me.

Blindingly fast, I lifted her off the ground and carried her all the way until her back struck the wall. With one quick movement, I raised her up and she flung her legs around to straddle my waist. Her hands were around my neck, while mine firmly clutched her butt to hold her there.

I thrust inside her.

Ramming hard, pounding fiercely, my anger dissipated. Fury fell away with each stroke inside her.

Mia surrendered in my arms, letting me ride her hard and fast, seemingly knowing this furious man fucking her needed his woman to find himself again, and only through her could there be any solace.

My gaze lowered to watch my slick cock, wet from her sex, slide in and out in endless thrusting. My hips pushed forward to raise the pleasure and find that sweet spot inside her.

She whispered, "I need this too."

"Mia," I breathed her name like an incantation.

"Harder, Cameron," she moaned. "I need it harder."

Pounding her pussy, delivering these rapid-fire thrusts, I pressed her further against the wall for leverage.

Her teeth embedded in my shoulder and she came. Her sex owned mine and sent me over with her. This all-consuming pleasure of warmth surrounded me and soaked her.

"I can't be without you," she said.

I lowered her to the ground and stepped back. "Mia, if I change?"

She rested her palm on my cheek. "I'll always be here for you."

Mia strolled over to the window and yanked off the gold braid tassel that held the long green velvet drape back. It tumbled closed, darkening the room.

She brought the tassel back to me and offered it up. "Master."

I took it from her and caressed the fine braid between my finger and thumb.

She held her wrists together. "I'll always find you."

Firmly, I weaved the braid around her wrists, binding her, sending her into subspace.

My gaze rose to meet hers. "This is not my home. You are."

Within seconds, I'd perched on the end of the bed and she sat on my lap with her back to me, her thighs straddling, her sex accepting my length eagerly.

Grasping her by the throat, I demanded, "You will watch."

A moan escaped her lips as her gaze met mine in our reflection, and then she lowered her eyes to watch how exposed she was, her thighs spread wide, the full view of my cock disappearing inside her sex. Her sensual glide hid me once more, then she pushed herself up slightly to allow the tip to rest at her entrance before she plunged once more, repeating her motion again and again, thighs shuddering, pussy clenching, her nipples erect as I brushed my fingers over them to tweak, squeeze, and pinch.

"Imagine being watched like this?" I teased.

"Oh," she moaned wantonly.

"Everyone staring at your cunt," I whispered huskily. "Wondering how you taste, Mia."

She plunged violently, riding me ever faster.

I'd never seen her so alighted by my words before. Her secret predilection glared, indicated by those soaking wet thighs, her feverish breathing, and her muscles milking me with a crazed need.

A master's true worth was his ability to lead his sub to the place where she felt safe enough to share her secrets, and, should she prove ready, see them realized for her.

I'd never be willing to share her. I'd always known that—

But showcase her?

"Be still," I demanded and reached low, easing apart her folds, and again my gaze found hers in the mirror. "See—" I tapped her clit —"How ready you are. How wet? Tight. Are you willing to allow others to share in the beauty of witnessing this delicate flower being fucked?"

"I want that," she cried out.

"Nice and still now," I said, flicking her clit slowly. "Watch, Mia."

Jaw gaping, lips pouting, her eyes traced the way I used a fingertip to circle her clit, slow and sure, on and on, until her eyelids became heavy as she tranced out.

She threw her head back and came hard, her orgasm causing her to shudder violently.

"Ride me, Mia," I ordered.

She obeyed, rising and falling, rising and falling. Her eyes squeezed shut only to burst open again and watch her wild and untamable reflection, cascading blonde locks whipping from side to side. Her pleasure grew so intense she became frenzied. Her sex beat my cock, and, leaning back on the bed, I used my hands for leverage so I could buck my hips and pummel her the rest of the way.

We collapsed on the bed.

Freeing her from that braid, caressing her wrists, I planted a kiss to each one.

I pulled her up and maneuvered her body until I was spooning her.

"The things you do to me," she said in a rush.

"You liked that, sweet sub?"

"Did you mean what you said?"

"About what?"

"Having people watch us?"

"I thought it might turn you on."

"I was already turned on."

"Good point."

She shifted to better look at me. "It's one of my fantasies."

"You've never told me this before?"

"I was embarrassed."

"With me?"

"Yes, Cameron, I know you're the master of the dark arts and all that—"

"All that?"

She settled against me again. "I want to dabble."

A word Richard had probably used around her. It was too cosmopolitan for her.

Mia looked up at me. "I want everyone to see you claim your submissive."

I kissed her nose. "Already have."

Her head rested on my chest.

"Let's discuss it another time," I said. "Perhaps when things have calmed a little."

"I want it."

I needed to explore the truth in those words. Her wanting to please me could even overrule her own happiness.

"You know the rules, Mia. The dom leads the play when he knows without question his sub is primed for that level."

"I'm excited,' she whispered.

"Let's discuss it another time."

"You don't think I'm ready?"

"I want you to do it for you. Stage work is an intense experience. A heavy scene. It must be carefully crafted."

She raised her head to look at me. "When you deem me ready then?"

"I'll consider it."

She beamed at me. "Your parents have swans."

"Yes."

"Do they bite?"

She made me smile. "Peck."

"Of course, silly."

"Either way it hurts."

"Did you get pecked?"

"Chased, once."

"They're pretty."

"Until they open their six foot wingspan and come at you hissing."

"It's funny, isn't it? How those of us on the outside of these big houses look in and think you all have idyllic lives."

"It's idyllic now." I pushed myself up the headboard and she snuggled against my chest as I reached over and brought the file onto my lap.

"What's that?" she said sleepily.

"Some light reading. Rest your head on my lap."

Mia nuzzled down and she let out a sigh of contentment.

I flipped open to the first page.

CHAPTER 11

MY HAND RESTED on Shay's shoulder. "Okay, buddy?"

He sat squarely at the dining room table and leaned back to look at me. "Yes, thank you." He gave me a knowing look of reassurance.

We'd all dressed for lunch, with the men wearing blazer and slacks, a formality for the Coles, and Mia wearing a deep blue chiffon dress.

Henry complained by tugging his collar and feigning he was choking to death until Mom scolded him.

Shay tried to defuse the strain. "You have a lovely pool, Mrs. Cole."

"Thank you, Shay," she said.

I took the seat beside his and smiled over at Mom. "You look lovely."

"Thank you, Cameron." She went on to inform us how she'd chosen the theme of the pool from the Trianon Palace Versailles, when she'd spent a week at the Waldorf Astoria last year with Willow.

Willow shared how she'd like to get married there.

"It's right next to the Palace of Versailles gardens," said Willow. "Where we could get our photos taken."

"You're getting married in a church," said Mom.

"The Waldorf would be for the reception."

"This imaginary husband does not exist," said Dad. "Not yet

57

anyway. Before you get your brothers interrogating you on the matter, Willow."

"I'm sure he'll be quite perfect when she does find him," said Henry with a hint of sarcasm.

"Something you want to share, Willow?" I said, amused.

She placed her napkin on her lap. "You'll be the first to know, Cam. Daddy shall have to wait until I've had you check him out and analyze him. And you too Shay." She beamed over at him.

Shay grinned at her. "Of course."

"Let's worry about all that when it happens," said Dad, who was seemingly already over it.

Right now he had the weight of the world on his shoulders, so considering this he was doing remarkably well.

I'd purposefully sat Mia between Henry and I, both of us flanking her in a show of protection from Mom's critical glare.

Lunch was served on fine china plates with gold trimming. Spring vegetables and lovage broth with poached guinea fowl served as our appetizer. For our main course, Confit gressingham duck leg was elegantly presented with truffle potatoes and asparagus. Dessert was Crème Brulee, and I refused to make eye contact with Mia as we ate our memorable sugared vanilla pudding that brought a smile to our lips.

We all declined the offer of wine, except Mom, who knocked back half a bottle of a Coche-Dury Les Perrieres like water.

This four course meal was usual for a weekend at home, delivered by waiters donning starched white uniforms and silently attending to our every need. What I wouldn't have given for a hamburger eaten in a quiet room tucked away in the library, where I could continue reading that monster of a file. This felt like time wasted.

Tension hung beneath the surface, and we all played our part to feign this was lunch as usual and on Monday my father wouldn't be clearing out his office. A legacy destroyed.

"So, Mia," said Mom, "any decisions on your future?"

Mia glanced over to me for support.

"Mia has a couple of exciting opportunities," I said. "Right now she's deciding on a career in fashion or psychology."

"Don't you need a degree for either one?" said Mom.

"I'm going to study at university," said Mia.

"Don't people usually decide on this kind of thing while at boarding school?"

I threw Mom a stare that told her to pull back on her cruelty.

"Actually, I'm trying to convince Mia to come on board at Cole Tea." Henry smiled warmly at her.

Dad scoffed. "Not sure any Cole will be welcome after Monday."

"She's not a Cole," said Mom.

"Not yet," I said with a smile that hit its mark, judging from the way Mom settled back in her chair.

"Still," Mom said, "trying to catch up on an education squandered is a little lacking in foresight."

Mia's face blushed wildly and her gaze fell to her lap.

"Give us a moment, please." I directed the last waiter out of the room.

"Mom," I said. "Enough."

"Well at least you didn't scold me in front of my staff, Cameron. You may have forgotten every last social grace I taught you, but that one still holds."

"What are you talking about?" I said.

"I'm sorry," whispered Mia. "This is my fault."

"Mia, please," I warned her and my focus returned to Mother.

"Had you and your brother not gone off and pursued your own agenda, you would have been here for your father. None of this would have happened."

"Not necessarily true," said Dad.

"You've needed them now more than ever."

"Henry was destined for West Point," said Dad. "Don't bring him into this."

"Perhaps we should discuss this in private, Mom," said Henry.

She threw her napkin on the table. "Cameron, you chose to live in another state and pursue a career that has no value."

"I profoundly help my patients."

"So could any other doctor," she said. "You make it sound like no one else could do what you do."

"Please," said Dad. "We've been over this."

"I'm here in whatever capacity you need me. I've handed my clinic over to my co-workers for now. I'm not going home until Cole Tea is back in your hands, Dad."

"There should only be family here," said Mom. "Shay's family. He's more than proven his worth."

"If you'll excuse us." I stood and grabbed Mia's hand.

Henry reached out for my arm and pulled me down. "I was blindfolded when they did it."

I sat back down and turned to look at him, my emotions swirling.

Henry stared at Mom. "Took their time doing it too. Ripped out my fingernails one by one."

"Oh, dear God," said Mom. "Cameron, say something."

Henry raised his hand. "No, you need to hear this, Mom, and you too, Dad. It was early in the morning. I remember like it was yesterday." He stared at his hands. "Even though they've grown back, I can still feel the pain."

"Not at lunch, dear," said Mom.

"Victoria." Dad silenced her with a glare.

She settled down, we all did, honoring Henry's memories with the silence it deserved.

"My captors messed with my mind," he said. "They warn you about this at West Point, but nothing can truly prepare you. The terrorists tell you you're being exchanged for one of their prisoners and you calm a little. Let your guard down. Then, when you've willingly walked into the interrogation room, they sit you down and play loud music for three days and three nights straight. If you manage to drift off, they kick you just to make sure you don't get any sleep. I was holding up pretty well. Wouldn't tell them anything."

I poured a glass of water and slid it over to him.

Henry stared at it. "You lose faith in humankind. You learn never to trust again. When you come back home, there's this sense everyone's lying to you. You can't shake it. The paranoia. I question everything, every conversation, every interaction, and every phone call." He looked at Mom.

"It was terrible what they did to you, son," she whispered.

"You're missing the point," he said. "I was destined to stay in that cabin in Big Bear for the rest of my life. When this one here turned up." He pointed to Mia. "I was rude to her at first. Tried to scare her off. Keep her at arm's length. But she wouldn't relent. Talked her way in and spent her time listening to me ramble on about nothing. She renewed my faith in the human condition. Made me believe in unconditional love again. Do you want to know how?"

Mom's gaze fell on Mia.

Henry looked over at Mia with affection. "Because she knew that Cameron and I needed each other. That you, Mom, needed me. And I needed all of you. That the only lies were the ones I'd been telling myself. That it was not okay living in isolation. Missing out on life. Alone. Mia Lauren turned up out of nowhere and saved my life from the futile experience it had become."

I took Mia's hand in mine and squeezed it.

"Well that's quite a revelation," said Dad. "We appreciate you sharing that with us."

Shay scratched his head. "Lunch really was delicious."

"Yes," said Mom weakly. "We have a new chef."

"We're lucky to have you in the family, Mia," said Willow.

Mom rose, pushing her chair back, its legs scraping the marble floor.

Our stares fell on her.

All of us recoiled over what she was going to say next.

She rounded the table and gestured to Mia. "Please stand."

"Mom," I said.

"It's okay," said Mia softly and pushed herself to her feet, turning to face my mother.

I rose and stood directly behind Mia, ready to say what was necessary to protect her.

Mom gripped Mia by her shoulders and stared at her. "I've got you in the wrong room, Mia. I'll have the staff move you."

"If you like, Mrs. Cole. But it really is a lovely room. I'm very grateful."

"We'll put you in the Windsor Suite," said Mom. "Now, if you'll excuse me, I must powder my nose."

When she left, Shay swapped a wary glance with me.

"Windsor Suite." Dad mused to himself. "Reserved exclusively for visiting dignitaries."

"I don't want to be a bother," whispered Mia.

Dad smiled at her. "You're my son's Magnum opus, Ms. Lauren."

I suppressed a moan of embarrassment for her.

CHAPTER 12

DAMN.

"You googled it, didn't you?" I said.

Mia dropped her phone to her side and turned away.

"Answer me." I kept my voice low so Henry and Shay, who were waiting for us inside the library, couldn't overhear.

Mia stepped away from the door. "Opus? How embarrassing, Cameron. Your girlfriend is your finest piece of work."

"Did I not tell you that once myself?"

"Yes, but I didn't think everyone else would think it too. That they'd all know because of you I'm now able to walk with my head held high and not be ashamed of who I once was. A girl from Charlotte who knows nothing other than what you've taught me. A common—"

"I told you never to refer to yourself in that manner."

"Why? Because the truth embarrasses you?"

"Do you honestly believe that Jesus, or Gandhi, or Buddha cared about how to hold a glass by the stem? Or cared about what is considered acceptable by a class of people who worship money?" I pulled her into a hug. "No Mia, the wisest and kindest men who ever walked the earth didn't give a damn about such superficiality because they were too busy trying to save the world from itself."

"Everyone can see I don't belong."

I pressed her up against the wall. "Have you ever once

considered that I'm your Opus, Mia?"

"How do you mean?"

"I'm your finest work."

"I changed you?"

"Of course."

"Your world is so different."

"That's why I avoid it."

She shrugged in agreement.

"Mia, you've ruined my reputation."

She suppressed a smile.

"I may not be able to prevent the monsters from reaching us, but what I can do is teach you how to deal with the fuckers when they turn up. And if that's what you being my opus means, then so be it."

She flung herself into my arms. "Oh, Cameron, I need you so much. It scares me how much."

"I know."

"I love you."

"You just melted my mother's heart. An accomplishment not to be taken lightly. She's moving you to the Windsor Suite, for goodness sake. Let's just take a moment to celebrate." I waved my fist in triumph. "This might be as good as it gets. Let's savor it."

She relaxed a little. "It helps seeing your parents approve of me."

"Well at least someone in this house has made the grade." I tapped her arm. "Come on. We have work to do."

I opened the door to the library and gestured for her to go on ahead, then I followed her in.

Shay and Henry rose to their feet to greet us.

Discreetly, I took a moment to check on Henry. After that dark reflection he'd just shared with us at lunch, I needed to know he was handling all this. His body language revealed he was holding up. His subconscious coping strategies had been effective. His playful banter with Shay was also a positive sign.

No matter how many times I told Henry how remarkable he was, it never seemed to sink in with him. Such was my brother's nature.

"So, what's the plan?" said Shay.

I strolled over to the central table, rifled through the drawer, and removed several permanent black markers. "We're going to gather intelligence. Profile each individual on the board."

"Find out their weak spot?" said Shay.

"Strengths, weakness, where they live, how many children they have, their interests, work history, affairs—"

"So we can blackmail them?" asked Shay.

I picked up one of the pens. "No, we play by the rules. That way after the vote we have re-secured their loyalty. We must shore up the foundation so this never happens again." I strolled over to the far wall and pulled off the pen lid. "You're going to bring me the information and I'm going to identify areas that will be used to sway the vote."

"I'm not sure I know enough about business," said Mia.

"Not a problem. Let's bring you up to speed. We have ten board members. Their responsibility is to protect the shareholders assets and make sure the return on their investments are profitable. The board holds a great deal of power. They recommend stock splits, approve the finances, and have the power to promote a merger or acquisition. Change their mind and we change the vote."

"Well that seems simple enough," said Shay sarcastically.

"It's all Mia needs to know for our purpose," I said.

"So after we've gathered all this," said Shay. "We call them?"

"Visit them." I glanced at my watch.

"But what if we sway them this year and next year this happens again?" said Shay.

"Dad's reassured me his old attorney put an addendum in place to prevent it happening again."

"Old?" said Shay.

"As in just died."

"Suspiciously?"

"Heart attack on the golf course."

"Another good reason never to play golf," said Henry.

"What's the first reason?" asked Shay.

"I hate golf."

Mia sat up. "What kind of addendum?"

"I've yet to find it," I said.

"It's in that contract you were reading?"

"Yes."

"Dad gave you a contract to read?" asked Henry.

"It's five hundred pages long. Want to take a look?"

"I'm good," he said.

I smiled and shook my head. "So, here's where we start..."

We used the back wall to write the board members' names and beneath it left a vertical space where we'd add in details. We set up three laptops found around the house and also utilized the desktop. We worked fast, starting with addresses, financial status, family members, and political preferences from voting records. We even managed to obtain medical data from their Cole Tea policies. Shay's hacking skills came in handy on all fronts.

As Mia, Henry, and Shay began notating the information under each name, I sat in the corner watching footage, including interviews that had been conducted over the years, studying every perspective of each person.

I was so engrossed in a YouTube video of board member Leonard Maybury that I hadn't noticed my mom enter. Rubbing the tiredness from my eyes, I realized she was standing stock-still, gaping at the wall's graffiti.

"I'll paint over it," I told her.

She left and closed the door behind her.

After swapping a wary stare with Henry, I went back to the screen.

Twenty minutes later, Mom returned. She carried a tray with four mugs of coffee and proceeded to hand them out, adding milk and sugar as needed.

She smiled fondly at Mia as she prepared her beverage.

Mia was her usual kind and appreciative self, showing Mom there were no hard feelings.

Now it was my turn to gape, and on Mia's subtle gesture, I closed my mouth.

Mom strolled over to the wall.

"He made me do it," murmured Henry with a glint of mischief.

"Leonard Maybury." She rested a fingertip by his name. "His parents were German immigrants. He studied business at Wharton. We took a holiday together a year ago with his wife Sally in Bavaria."

I rose to my feet and headed over. "That's good, Mom. Keep going."

Her eyes glinted with warmth. "Leonard experienced bankruptcy in his late twenties. His first business went under due to his over-leveraged hotel and casino business in New Orleans."

I pointed to his name. "His wife?"

She gave a nod and held her hand out for the pen. "We're on the same charity committee. Sally's religious."

"Catholic?"

"Yes."

"Do you get along with her?"

"Yes, I like her."

I picked up the spare marker and drew a line through his name. "He's last. Just in case."

"Just in case?" asked Shay.

"We run out of time," I said.

Mom frowned. "But he went through something similar to what your dad's going through right now."

"Yes," I said, "and he cheated his way back to success. He'll be hard to extract empathy from."

She frowned. "You're going to visit them?"

"After I've finished profiling."

"I should go with you."

"I imagined you phoned everyone?"

"Yes."

"They're closing ranks."

"But there isn't enough time to visit everyone," she said. "You only have a day."

I nodded. "That's why we need to be precise."

"Like a laser beam," said Shay.

"Look at this, Cameron." Mia had a file opened in front of her. I headed on over.

"What is that?" asked Mom.

"It's the list of signatures," said Mia. "Where each board member—"

"Stabbed us in the back," said Mom.

Mia pointed. "This is interesting. Look at Mr. Malt's signature. It's a little shaky and looks nothing like the one here from two years ago. Do you think someone else signed it?"

I dragged the list over and compared it to where Douglas Malt had previously signed his name for a memo.

"Perhaps he has arthritis now?" said Mia. "That would account for it."

"Your dad did mention Douglas hadn't attended the last few meetings," said Mom. "He conducts all business dealings from home. His wife was his secretary back in the day."

"Can his signature be voided?" asked Shay.

"That would win a vote back," said Henry.

I opened Douglas Malt's file. "He lives in Greenwich." I headed back over to the wall and scribbled an asterisk beside his name. "Let's pay him a visit first."

"What is that?" Mom looked horrified.

She'd caught sight of the medical conditions I'd written beneath each name, tucked away beneath the list of family members, including grandchildren.

"Brendon Smith had a heart attack a year ago," I said. "We're making a note of medical records too. I need a complete profile."

"How did you find that out?"

"We might have a hacker in our midst," I said.

"That's not legal," she said.

"We're using what we find for the good of Cole Tea."

"If you must," she said weakly.

Henry arched his brows.

"I need the key to this room," I said. "No one, and I mean no one, enters here without my permission."

Mom's stare swept across the wall. "I'll personally paint over it when we're done."

"Now let's not go too far, Mom," said Henry. "We don't want there to be a crack in the space-time continuum."

It was good to see her laugh.

CHAPTER 13

"YOUR BEAUTY, IT haunts me," I whispered.

Mia blushed. "Such a romantic."

"I'm serious. Can't drag my eyes off you."

"We need to focus."

"I'm focused." Reluctantly I pulled my hand away from hers. "Perhaps wearing FMBs wasn't a good idea."

"You bought them for me."

"Technically, Penny did." I yawned.

"Did you get any sleep last night?"

I leafed through the coffee table book featuring old photos of New York.

The answer was *no,* but Mia didn't need to know I'd been up all night, nose deep in that document, refusing to give up until I'd found what I was looking for. Whatever it was meant to be.

I was going on forty-eight hours without sleep.

We'd been invited in by Mrs. Malt and had been escorted into the sitting room and left waiting for her to go and arrange refreshments.

The minimalist décor reflected a couple who loved to travel and hinted this wasn't the family home. White walls, soft browns, and elegant furniture reflected an older couple's taste, along with those photos of grandchildren, some graduating college, others venturing into impressive careers. The Malts had a fighter pilot in the family, apparently. The young man's smile hid the horrors of a cruise ship at war.

The view of the city was stunning. The vibrant vista had yet to light up the night sky and reveal why so many loved New York.

My gaze returned to Mia.

"Why are you looking at me like that?" She smiled.

"I'm waiting for you to open those sliding doors, strip naked, and take a running jump into the pool."

"I need to remain professional, Dr. Cole."

"Pity."

"I'm sure Mrs. Malt wouldn't appreciate a naked woman doing laps."

"Might work," I said. "I'll tell her you're not getting out unless Doug overturns his vote. It may be considered one of my more genius manipulations."

Glancing at my phone, I beamed a smile.

Mia leaned over to look. "They overturned it?"

I'd sent Henry and Shay to Maurice Reiner's house, and they'd just confirmed they'd changed his mind.

That left us with nine votes to go.

Maurice's ex-forces background included him serving as a helicopter pilot when he was at Camp Bondsteel, the main base of the U.S. under KFOR command in Kosovo. Maurice had resigned his commission weeks after his father's unexpected death. He'd inherited his dad's estate, which included a news station and a dying newspaper. There was no doubt the bond between those who'd been in the military went deep, and Shay and Henry would have had the cards tipped in their favor for getting through to him, making Maurice a likely candidate to change his vote.

As was Doug Malt, who'd once been considered a close friend of my father's and had shared more fond memories with my family than any other member of the board.

Though he'd not been seen in public for the last few months, and as such we'd all suspected a major illness and chosen to ignore the ruse that he was on a worldwide lecturing tour.

The truth lay in what Mrs. Malt was willing to share.

She reappeared and sat in the armchair opposite. "Drinks are on their way."

"Thank you for seeing us on such short notice," said Mia. "We value your time."

She gave a nod of thanks. "Dr. Cole, how are your parents?"

"Fairing well, considering. Please, call me Cameron."

"Cameron." She pressed her hand to her chest. "Susan."

"This is Mia," I said. "Susan, it's good to see you again."

She gave a nod. "This is a pleasant surprise. I haven't seen you since the party your father threw for Henry after his graduation."

"Henry's actually out of the military now," I said. "He's joined the business."

"Doesn't time fly. It seems like only yesterday."

"It does."

"You two are so close."

"We are."

"And Willow? How is she?"

"Still obsessed with horses," I said. "No change there."

She sat back. "Did your father send you?"

Mia gestured our sincerity. "Whatever you tell us will not leave this room, Mrs. Malt. We promise."

"You have our word," I said.

She stared down, as though still unsure. "I'm so sorry how it all worked out."

"It's not over," I said. "There's still time."

"Everyone has signed it I'm afraid," she said.

"Mrs. Malt, may I speak with your husband?"

"He's resting."

"I really need to see him. My father's life's work is hanging in the balance."

She stared at the carpet and her gaze swept the floor.

"Mr. Malt has Alzheimer's?" said Mia softly.

Susan's gaze rose.

"We realize this is extraordinarily private," I said.

"We understand," said Mia. "We know how difficult this is."

"Understand?" said Susan.

"We empathize." I gestured to the stack of leather bound photo albums. "A visual aid?"

"If you'll excuse me," she said, standing. "I have family heading into town."

"Those visual aids do help in bringing him back to you, but what then?" I said softly. "His moments of clarity bring him distress. He's fully aware in that moment of his diagnosis."

"It's so hard," she whispered.

"I'm so sorry," said Mia.

"Who told you?"

"As a doctor…" I said. "Well, it's intuitive."

I left out we'd utilized Shay's hacking skills.

"You can't truly comprehend what the last year has been like," said Susan.

"When Doug's present, you savor those few minutes," I said.

She conceded with a nod.

I leaned forward. "There's new clinical research results coming out of Zurich. Their findings are extraordinary. The drug has just been approved. If you like, I can arrange for Doug to receive it."

She sat back down, her face marred with confusion. "With Doug's connections, you'd have thought it would be easy."

"The FDA is a wary gatekeeper."

"The trials have proven effective?"

"Yes."

She shook her head woefully. "The one man in my life who could understand those results and make the decision based on his experience. Maybe run his own tests."

"Doug's a brilliant scientist," I said.

"He was."

I'd known him as a quiet man, obsessed with medical research, having married into money yet determined to leave his own mark on the world. A friend of my father's who'd come onto the board at his behest to inspire loyalty among the others.

"I'll have the medication delivered by a specialist in the field," I said. "They'll guide you through the process and measure its efficacy."

"You'll do that?"

"Of course."

"You always did prefer medicine."

I sat back. "Yes, taking care of my patients became a priority. Taking care of their families who needed me just as much has consumed my time. I'm sure you're finding such dedication from your own doctors reassuring at this time?" I placed my hand on my heart. "I'm still my father's son."

She gave a nod. "Of course you are."

"There was a time when I lost my one true love," I said. "Couldn't have her. She was out of reach and there was nothing I could do or say to put that right. I felt like I was drowning, and I suppose in many ways I was. There was no way to get her back. Or so I believed. Those were the darkest days of my life."

And of my own making, I mused.

"What happened?" asked Susan.

"Fate intercepted. I got her back."

"I'm happy for you."

I rested my elbows on my knees. "When it comes to understanding what losing the love of your life feels like, I've lived it."

"No one can ever know," she muttered. "His work would be jeopardized."

Mia shot me a concerned look.

"You forged his signature," I said. "Doug would never have signed that contract."

"The other members of the board were very persuasive."

"They called a private meeting?"

"Last Thursday."

"Who set it?"

"Remy Parker."

I knew little of him other than his suspected connections with another tea conglomerate out of China.

"When I got to the meeting I realized your father hadn't been invited. It was a coup."

"You were concerned if you spoke up your husband would be put in the spotlight?"

"The last few years of his work will be compromised," she said. "His latest scientific developments will be scrutinized. His latest drug threatened and quite possibly pulled from the market. It saves so many lives."

"PolFlexa," I said. "Limited side-effects and its efficacy in treating Glioblastomas is groundbreaking."

"Doug knew," said Susan, "He recognized his early symptoms. So he took himself out of the lab and entered early retirement. The plan was to remain on your father's board long enough to provide some space between leaving work."

"Create no suspicion," I said.

"He so loves your father."

"Dad did mention that of all the members it was Doug's betrayal that most hurt him."

"It was all so overwhelming," she said. "Remy framed it as being best for the shareholders."

"Did you see the new advertising campaign?" I said dryly.

"That bad?" She suppressed a grin.

"Oh yes. Cole's a classic brand that could do with moving forward, but in a more refined way."

We spent the rest of the morning talking about Doug, about them and how they met, sharing stories of her long and happy marriage. We talked about the business and what it had meant to both her and her husband to be involved in Cole Tea, as well as the company's philanthropic pursuits.

She brushed off a speck of dust from her pants. "Your father has seemed a little overwhelmed lately, what with opening offices in San Francisco and his plans to expand to L.A. I believed this may actually help him. Nudge him into retirement."

I gave a nod. "He's a good man."

"You want me to talk frankly?"

"Yes, of course."

"You and your brother are only now interested in Cole Tea? At the eleventh hour."

"We believed there'd always be time."

She lowered her gaze.

"We know you forged Doug's signature," I said. "Reverse your vote."

"Is this a veiled threat?"

"A promise that I'll commit fully to my father's business."

"Leave medicine?"

Mia shifted beside me, but I refused to look at her. I didn't want her to see my conflict. Some part of me believed there was no saving Cole Tea and any promise made would dissipate with the fall of an empire. Yet a certainty lingered that I had what it took to reverse a hostile attack.

There came a sense that every moment of my life had led me here.

Susan looked beyond the window. "With you and Henry in

73

charge I believe the business would stand a chance." Her eyes met mine again. "Dedicate your life fully to Cole Tea."

"Without question."

She gave a nod of acceptance. "Now all you have to do is convince the others."

CHAPTER 14

"CAMERON?" whispered Mia.

"Just give me a moment."

The limousine pulled away smoothly. Our driver turned up the air conditioning just as I'd asked. Mia snuggled in, her body warm and soft against my mine. I focused on the passing view, immersed in self-analysis.

The town car drove us farther into the city.

"Do you want to talk about it?" Mia broke the silence.

My thoughts scattered, trying to make sense of the last forty-eight hours.

"Don't be frightened of the future," she said.

"I'm cautious."

"Remember what you once told me? Our subconscious naturally guides us to our future."

"Sounds like I was trying to get into your panties."

She playfully thumped my arm. "You've taught me so much. That we must trust the path we're on."

What if this is the wrong fork in the road?

"I know what you need."

I arched a brow.

She pushed herself up and straddled me. "This is the best way to be in the present moment." She waved her hand. "The future isn't going anywhere."

"Just what are you insinuating, Ms. Lauren?"

She glanced over to the divider.

"He can't hear us," I reassured her. "No one can see in. The windows are tinted."

"I thought that was illegal?"

"We have friends in high places." I reached below her skirt and slipped a finger between her hip and thong and snapped it off.

She feigned a gasp.

"That was your fault," I said.

"How?"

"You wore FMBs."

"You wrote on the box 'wear me.'"

"Sure that note was for you?"

She crushed her lips to my mouth and swirled her tongue against mine. Her passion alighting my nerves and sent me reeling.

I pulled her closer, kissing with the deepest affection. My hand slid to her sex and I plunged two fingers inside her. My thumb encircled her clit.

Mia rode my hand deliriously.

The scent of her hair, her soft skin brushing against me, her aliveness, and the way her golden locks tussled over her shoulders and breasts—all this soothed me.

She stilled, shuddering against my chest, mewling as she came.

Then fell against me, nestling into my neck.

When Mia finally recovered, she slid down onto the floor between my legs, kneeling before me, reaching for my zipper. She freed me from my pants, my hardness responding to her firm grip that worked me with an insistence I hadn't realized I needed. At my feet, she provided the kind of affection I could never live without.

She took me in her mouth and this ache in my cock intensified, causing my head to fall back and my mind to lose all thoughts. All I knew was her. Her mouth, her tongue, her perfectly placed hands possessing me.

I'd been so distracted lately I'd hardly treated Mia as my submissive.

Her training had been put on hold during these last few days of chaos. Though my domination of her would always remain a constant, as it should be, she thrived beneath my power, as though knowing I'd always be here for her, helped her find the freedom to make her own way.

I adored her quirkiness, or her obsession with water, or the way she didn't seem to realize how cruel this world really was. She'd experienced more than her fair share of pain, but forgiveness came easily for her. My sweet, incandescent, Mia.

She used that trick, strumming the under head with flicks and licks, cupping my balls in her delicate hand and squeezing. I reached low and eased my hand beneath her blouse until I'd caught her nipples between my thumb and index fingers and pinched, eliciting a moan that vibrated along my length.

God, how she knew me.

She eased my hands off her. "Relax."

Who was I to argue?

Resting back, I stared up and went with it, with her, my hips rocking, my balls begging for mercy.

Mia's beauty was distracting—the way her eyes caught mine, the way she sucked firmer with pouty lips controlling me, taking me all the way to the back of her throat.

"I'm going to come, Mia," I said huskily.

She let out a protracted moan of pleasure, and when I came, I came hard, filling her mouth and marveling at how she swallowed without missing a drop.

My eyes closed, my body soothed with relaxation, I felt her tuck me away. Then she placed soft kisses on my chest. Her lips pecked my chin and cheek.

I grinned, eyelids still closed, sleep luring me.

Finally…

I cupped my eyes for a beat when my iPhone chimed its assault, then I reached inside my jacket. It had gone to voicemail.

Uncertainly spiked in my veins as I read Shay's text: *Get here now. We have a situation.*

I dialed his number.

"Cam." His voice sounded tense, hushed.

"What's going on?"

"Blackwood's wife's into skeet shooting."

A loud crack, a ricochet, and I pulled the phone away from my ear.

"Cam, she's in the garden—"

"Henry?"

"He's locked himself in a bathroom."

My gut twisted in knots.

"Some kind of flashback I think," he said.

Another shot—

"Is he talking?" I said.

"Radio silent."

Shit.

"Blackwood thinks we've left," said Shay. "I'm assuming you want everyone to think Henry's fine, considering Blackwood's vote is riding on the competency of the Cole brothers."

"Did Henry show any signs of stress?"

Had I missed them?

"No, none. Cam, Blackwood reassured us he'd think about reversing his vote. We have him. We're sure of it. But the situation's now fragile."

"I'm on my way."

"I'll find something to pick the lock."

"Keep him calm."

"You don't think Henry will hurt himself, do you?"

"Why do you say that?"

"I've never seen him like this."

"How?"

"Emotional."

Fuck it.

"Break the door down," I snapped.

Damn the consequences.

CHAPTER 15

THE CLAY DISK shattered, and the sound of another bullet hitting its mark echoed.

Shay had defied my order and found what he needed to pick the bathroom door. I found him sitting beside Henry. I'd watched a torn up Shay leave and knew that Mia, who waited outside, would comfort him. This was hard on Shay too, having witnessed firsthand what Henry had gone through after serving right beside him. Shay had his own scars.

But they were nothing like Henry's.

He sat on the floor in the corner with his arms wrapped around his legs.

I slid down the wall and sat beside him. "Blackwood's wife has too much free time. She's taking a break from shopping in Niemen Marcus to shoot clay pigeons in the garden."

He stared at his hands as though all answers were waiting to be realized.

"Imagine how the koi in their pond feel?" I squeezed his arm.

Following his gaze, I too studied the red damask wallpaper. Farther up hung a print of a watercolor. In any other circumstances, those blue and green pastels would have been comforting.

"Talk to me," I said.

Another shot rang out.

Henry patted his jacket down and I wondered if he was feeling for a pistol he didn't have.

"Lost something?" I said.

"Phone." He gestured. "In my pocket."

His coms—a good soldier was never without communication.

I'd sent Shay and Mia to go find Mrs. Blackwood and get her and her weekend buddies to stop. I didn't care what it took. They could grab the gun out of her hands for all I cared.

"I'm okay," he whispered.

"Yes, yes you are."

Beads of perspiration spotted his brow, his upper lip. His hands fisted into balls. "You were there," he stuttered. "You saw what it was like."

But I'd never served in uniform. The circumstances of my week in the Middle East were the result of being part of the team rescuing him.

Seeing Henry like this was tearing me apart.

He smiled weakly. "I think that was my first flashback."

I reasoned this was good. A clarity I could work with.

"It's over now," I said.

"I'm okay." He threw me a reassuring smile.

"I know you are."

"It's just been a little intense lately."

"I've got this, Henry."

"I've been thinking."

"Thinking?"

"About everything. Cole Tea, Dad's expectations—"

"He knows we're giving this our best."

"Am I? Really?"

"Yes, Henry, you've not stopped since we landed."

"You've not stopped."

Stretching my legs out before me, I was ready to follow where he was leading.

"I'm meant to be the future CEO," he whispered.

"You are."

"Then why are you masterminding every move we make?"

"You're utilizing the skills of your team."

"Don't patronize me, Cam. You know your handle on all this is better than mine."

"That's up for debate. Time will tell."

"I still have so much personal shit to work through."

"We'll work through it together. Simple. You and me chatting over a beer. Righting the world as we did as boys."

"It's meant to be me." He shifted to face me. "I'm the prodigal son, me. I was the one destined to leave the military and continue the family name. Take the business to the next level. Instead, where have I been the last few years? In a self-imposed prison weighed down with guilt..."

"Guilt?"

"For living such a privileged life. For these opportunities."

"We were born into this."

"Many of my boys didn't make it," he muttered. "I pledged to protect them, keep them safe."

"Think of the ones you did save?"

"Why me? Why do I get to live and they didn't?"

"Henry,—"

"The smell of diesel at a gas station," he muttered. "Takes me right back."

I had my nightmare infested memories too. That flight out to join the mission.

A desert dryness, the low hum of a C-130 cargo plane, the controlled chaos of finalizing a drop point.

I'd leaped from a plane into the blackness with a sixty pound pack strapped to my back in the grueling heat. During those few days of training, I'd hardly slept, being fraught with worry after that debriefing, which was delivered with the kind of preciseness I'd rather not have heard. Not until we'd gotten him out.

I'd been the one to continue Henry's torment, hours after Shay and his men had freed him and then slaughtered his captors.

What had followed was hours of hellish questions unleashed in a camouflaged tent. Military doctors closed his wounds while I stood by, ready to open the ones that couldn't be seen.

Despite his reassurance I'd done the right thing, us sitting in a bathroom together revealed otherwise.

"Don't," he snapped.

"Don't want?"

"I know you. Don't blame yourself."

I marveled at his insight.

"I willingly signed up," he said.

His saving grace had been he'd not turned to alcohol but art, painting up a storm in that cabin. I'd been the only privileged one to see his work. Renderings of the darkest times. Insight into a psyche. Those paintings were now preserved in my Beverly Hills home.

"You were willing to give your life for your men" I said. "That's profound, Henry."

"You don't expect to come home and be pointed at by strangers, or overhear their whispers that I'm the guy back from the war who's lost his mind."

"Henry, you're doing amazing."

"CEO?" He gave a nod. "Stuck in an office day after day?"

"It'll be fun."

He scoffed. "Says the man who's resisted this since birth."

"So far, so good."

"Your eyes lit up when you profiled those board members. Each time you discovered their motivations, you were positively high on adrenaline. You were made for this. You relish every second."

"So do you."

"Maybe what we've resisted all this time is really what we want."

"There's a mind fuck."

"Of which you're the expert."

We laughed and I felt the tension lessening.

The gunshots had ceased and I sent out a silent prayer of thanks.

Henry deserved his future, to rule as he'd always been destined to. How could we not spiral with the pressure of an empire resting on every action, every word?

I took a long, deep breath and began what I knew Henry needed right now—not to be led out of here, but for me to dedicate this time to seeing him through these unfolding moments, explore his thoughts, his doubts, his fears even.

I'd not been his therapist and had no idea just how much his experience had impacted his view of the world and his beliefs. War still haunted his days and nights and I refused to let its hold continue to impact him.

We talked, and I didn't care about the time, didn't care we

were still here.

We reminisced about our childhood, about those days being chased by swans in the garden, stealing snacks from the kitchen and running out of there triumphantly, and when we'd been packed off to boarding school, we'd both found comfort in each other.

We ruminated over Afghanistan and he revealed more to me. He was profoundly brave, a miracle of a man, and I vowed to do whatever he wanted to make him happy.

"Cam, what we are doing now is affecting us irrevocably," he said.

"I'm resigned to my fate."

"Which is?"

"To stand by your side, Henry. Support you in any way you need me."

"Why are we in a fucking bathroom?"

"Seriously?"

"Help me find Mrs. Blackwood so I can shove that rifle up her ass."

"Sounds like a plan. Let's get out of here."

We met Mia and Shay just outside and were greeted by the serenity we both needed from them—a warm smile, a hug—then we made our way down the hallway.

Mia grabbed my arm.

Halfway down stood Mr. Blackwood—

From his formidable expression, he too was wondering why we were still here.

Shay looked at me with a *good luck explaining this one, buddy.*

Blackwood's tweed suit and shotgun hinted he'd planned on firing off a few rounds himself. A sixty-year-old businessman whose run for presidency never made it to the White House. Now his retirement was filled with board meetings and enjoying the lecture circuit a man of his status savored.

I took a step forward. "I wanted to thank you for taking the time to hear what Henry had to say."

Blackwood gave a nod. "As I told your brother. I'll give you my answer tomorrow."

"We appreciate that," I said.

"Would you like to join us?" He raised his gun. "You boys

probably haven't shot off a weapon in years. I imagine you miss it."

Shay and Mia swapped a wary glance.

"Actually." I mentally ran through our options.

"I'd love to!" Mia burst out.

Our stunned gazes fell on her.

Shay reached for her arm.

"I'll meet you boys later." She pulled away and stood beside Blackwood, oozing enthusiasm. "Will your wife teach me?"

"She'd be delighted," said Blackwood with a smile.

"We'll send a car for you?" I said, proud of my girl.

Mia beamed, full of confidence. "This'll be fun."

Blackwood looked impressed. "Well at least one of you is game."

I gave her a nod—a silent message to call me should she need rescuing at any time. But having known Blackwood all my life, she'd be in good hands.

He led her off to join his wife in the garden.

CHAPTER 16

WE WERE AGAINST the clock and every vote counted and Mia knew this.

Shay had relayed to Mia how his meeting had gone and filled her in on Blackwood's concerns. Mia would have also known the responsibility of her intentions, the need to get this right.

My confidence in her was unwavering.

The driver parked our Bentley SUV outside Carnegie Deli on 55th St. and we picked up lunch, eating a selection of sandwiches and drinking Coke on the way to our next destination.

We pulled up outside board member Elliot Rice's home at one in the afternoon, and within the hour I'd had his guarantee he'd support us. Of course the offer of inviting his Yale educated grandson into the company and fast tracking him through to a senior position in marketing had sealed the deal.

The rest of the day went surprisingly smooth.

In between visits, I enjoyed watching Shay and Henry interact. Their friendship was based on trust and a past that few would ever understand.

Their stories had them both cracking up, and Shay lessened the tension of what had happened back at Blackwood's by having Henry talk about it.

His calmness had returned, and his self-awareness was a sign he was coping.

The car took us back to the Blackwood's.

We picked up Mia in the early evening. She appeared in a flurry of wayward hair and sun kissed cheeks, then flopped down in the seat opposite ours.

"Well?" I said.

"We hung out in the garden for a few hours with me trying to shoot those suckers," she said. "Nina, his wife, is on her third therapist, and we got some alone time to discuss Freud vs. Jung."

We all leaned forward, fascinated.

"And?" Henry nudged her on.

"Mrs. Blackwood seemed to have a lot of unresolved issues," said Mia. "So I just told her my opinion."

"Which was?" I said.

"That we really have to stop blaming our parents. If they were messed up and we know that, we can use what we learned to empower us."

"Fuck," snapped Henry.

"You told her about your dad?" I said quietly.

"And I told her how you worked out something so complex about my past from merely the evidence you'd gathered. That you saved me."

Her honesty, her ability to find no shame in her transparency, silenced us all.

She pointed to Henry. "And I told Mrs. Blackwood how brave you are. Didn't reveal anything personal. She knew a little of what happened to you from the papers. I told her you deserved a future at Cole Tea after dedicating your life to your country."

"Mia," I said. "That's…"

A reaction to such a monologue could have gone either way.

Mia beamed at us. "Blackwood's on board!"

We cheered together.

Henry collapsed back and laughed. "His wife persuaded him. Mia went through his wife."

"Of course," said Shay.

We were flying high from the exhilaration.

I'd surprisingly savored every second of analyzing the board members until I knew them better than they knew themselves, and proving just how much I could use this knowledge when with them. I'd never considered business to be this visceral. My work had always required a certain level of intuition, and until now any other profession had appeared dry and offered no similar challenge.

This revelation I was actually enjoying myself sent a thrill up my spine.

More importantly, it was good to see Henry calm again.

"We make an incredible team," I told them.

"You know, we'll be fighting over who gets Dad's office," said Henry.

"That'll be you, Henry. Cole Tea's new CEO."

"Fuck," he said. "That makes me sound so old."

"All we have to do now is capture the remaining three votes from board members living out of state," I said.

"They fly in tomorrow," said Henry. "Bastards, they're avoiding us."

"Not for long," I said.

CHAPTER 17

THE BOARD MEMBERS sat around the conference table, Doug Malt being the only one absent. They didn't need to know the reason.

My father sat at the head of the table with his fingers arched together in that familiar thoughtful pose. His frown now seemed a permanent fixture on that worn face. Dad was flanked by two members of his legal team. Henry sat at the other end, his gaze sweeping the room, having just delivered his speech about our vision for Cole Tea.

The response had been lukewarm. Betrayal lingered beneath the surface.

I stood at the back, and from this vantage I could read each expression. These men and woman who I'd won over yesterday weren't making eye contact now.

An undercurrent of tension.

A shift in their body language.

What was that? Guilt?

I expected this. After what they'd done, having to face my father again had to be grueling for them, but there was something else...

Fear?

David Atwood from New Orleans, Remy Parker based in Las Vegas, and Kat Leonard from Illinois were still on the fence with their decision. These three had flown in this morning and there had been no time to talk with them.

Silence lingered—

Through that long glass window, the dramatic vista of New York spread out.

Cole Tower boasted one of the best vantage points overlooking Central Park. The tallest building in Manhattan, situated just off 56th Street, it was lauded as one of the most noble of designs. It was built to withstand earthquakes and often featured in architectural magazines. Marble flooring, pristine fixtures, glass, mirrors strategically placed here and there, and its office and cubicles were spaciously designed to incorporate the atmosphere my dad had nurtured.

All one had to do was sip tea in the open café nestled in the atrium and savor the dramatic waterfall that cascaded down from ten floors. It fell into a carp filled glass pond lit up with gold lighting.

My dad's decadence proved he was a complex man. He lived simply, remained accessible to his staff, and knew their names. So no one was more surprised than me when I'd heard these men and woman had turned their backs on him.

Having consumed enough Cole coffee to keep a small city awake for a decade, and not having slept for God knows how many nights now, I used this intensity to maintain pressure on those final three by pacing around the room, circling them.

This kind of uncomfortable I'd become accustomed to when prying open a patient's psyche back in my L.A. clinic. I'd explored the depths of the human condition and not gotten lost along the way. That was easy. *This* was more challenging, and I was thriving under the pressure.

The scent of blood in the water.

We had them.

Henry had left them warily swapping gazes or merely staring into their beverages.

We'd provided a generous breakfast and served up Cole Tea and coffee in our signature mugs. Our logo on the cups, our crest on the napkins, our name hanging in the balance.

"Cameron." Dad gestured for me to speak.

Adrenaline forged through my veins and my heart raced with the excitement of closing this deal and putting this charade behind us.

Remy Parker broke the silence. "We were just as invested as you in taking Cole Tea forward."

Remy's use of past tense chilled my blood.

A seventy-year-old luxury casino owner who wore ill-fitting suits and had shifty eyes. I'd never liked him and could never understand how Dad had. I wanted him off the board.

"There must be changes," he said. "The foreign market has evolved. We're not keeping up."

"We agree that recent developments have altered the landscape," I said. "Which is why we brought on a dynamic team to implement changes. This man—" I pointed to my father— "removed the uncertainties for you and ensured each of you a return on your investments that far exceeded expectations. He knows this industry better than anyone. He's lived and breathed this company, and taken us into the twenty-first century with the kind of transition most Wall Street businesses could only dream about. Yes, laws change. Yes, we've had to face the evolution of both political and foreign policies. We've stood strong, kept our employees secure, provided scholarships for their children, and enviable healthcare for their families."

"Our competitors are winning," said Remy. "Adapt or die."

"There's villages in Nepal," I said. "Where my father drastically improved the mortality rates."

Dad had built on the infrastructure of the village, placed a medical facility in the town, and had not just cared about the product at any cost. He'd introduced a new Nepali tea into the market, producing the leaves in the eastern zones, and they were far superior to Darjeeling in flavor, appearance, and aroma. The method of processing the leaves produced at lower altitudes in the fertile plains provided an exceptional experience and was hailed by American tea connoisseurs as an award winning product.

"Nepali mothers once had to trek hundreds of miles on foot for medical care. No more, thanks to this man. Women with c-section scars, and the knowledge they may not make it, have been given the best chance of survival for them and their children by my father. You say adapt or die? This is adaption. Not just producing a product at any cost but taking in the human factor. Giving a damn about each and every employee and building loyalty. A legacy you once believed in."

David Atwood narrowed his gaze. "Shares have fallen. Faith in the business—"

"My father funded your run for senator," I snapped back. "Got you your seat."

"Of which I am eternally grateful."

"Your concerns are ill founded," I said. "The company is thriving."

"When was the last meeting you attended?" he snapped back.

I lowered my voice, resting my hand on his shoulder. "David, we need you to do the right thing today."

He sat back and gazed down.

We were close.

My focus turned to the remaining two members.

I inwardly flinched when I saw Shay gesturing to me through the glass. "Please, excuse me gentlemen."

Shay headed off to a nearby cubicle.

I followed him out.

"We have a situation," he said.

"Yes, we do. You just interrupted—"

"It's not good."

"Mia?"

Shay glanced over the cubicle to check we could talk. "There's been an incident back in L.A."

"For God sake, Shay, I'm in a fucking meeting—"

"Decker's dead."

"What?"

"My men were following him. He tried to evade us. He drove into a wall."

"Are you sure?"

"Quite sure."

"Adrian?"

"Turned up for work and then halfway through his shift disappeared."

"He's probably at the hospital."

Shay shook his head. "No, he identified his brother's body at the morgue then went off to work like nothing happened. Worked half his shift."

"Any sign of grieving?"

"No, just presented like your regular sociopath."

"Where the fuck did he go?"

"We're trying to locate him."

"Don't tell Mia."

"Of course."

"Fuck!" I caressed my forehead.

"We're watching his house."

"I have to get back."

"Breaking for lunch?" He nodded toward the conference room.

I turned and stared at the board members trickling out.

My hands fisted with tension and I walked briskly back toward them. "Ladies, gentlemen, we've not quite finished."

They ignored me and headed off, talking amongst each other, their arrogance raw and uncompromising.

Stunned, I watched them go.

Henry appeared in a panic and pulled me back inside the conference room.

"What just happened?" I said.

Henry shut the door. "We lost them, Cameron."

A wave of panic came over me. "How?"

Dad neared us and rested his hand on my shoulder. "They changed their mind on the vote."

My mouth went dry. "We had them."

Dad brought his phone to his ear. "They just delivered the news."

I stared at Henry, trying to read if I'd been too heavy handed, too arrogant to see I'd turned them off the deal. "What happened, Henry?"

"We don't know." He gestured to Dad's phone. "Who is it?"

Dad strolled over to the window to take the call.

His conversation was brisk, his tone defeated.

Dad hung up and turned to us. "That was Doug Malt's wife."

"What did she say?" asked Henry.

"Doug's wife discreetly mentioned—" Dad steadied himself on the back of a chair— "It's the kind of blackmail they can't fight."

"Blackmail?" The word burned my throat. "They threatened to leak her husband's condition to the press?"

"If that's what they've got on her," said Henry, "imagine what they have on the others."

Dad turned to me, his expression worn.

I swallowed hard, but this lump in my throat was destined to remain.

"I'll sign the contract this afternoon," said Dad. "Get legal to complete it."

Henry looked devastated.

"I'm sorry, boys." Dad turned and faced the glass.

CHAPTER 18

DAD STARED DEAD ahead, his words flowing like acid poured onto my heart. "*A leader has the right to be beaten, but never the right to be surprised.*"

He'd quoted Napoleon Bonaparte.

That truth rang in my ears.

And Adrian Herron was on the fucking loose.

I should have followed Dad when he left the conference room, but my feet wouldn't move.

Henry had already left.

The view of the city was vast and sweeping, and now I knew it had always been a threat in waiting, a warning I'd lied to myself that I had what it took to pull this off.

Swim backwards.

The words found me again in the loneliest place I'd ever stood. Our competitors had used the kind of tactics assembled in a dirty bomb—

Quick, ugly, and final.

Richard's voice boomed from my phone. "Cameron? Are you there?"

I stared down at my cell, realizing I'd dialed his number.

"Cam?"

"Where are you?" I said.

"Driving. Needed to clear my head."

"Skydiving?"

"On my way to the pick up now."

"Be careful."

"Always. You need to join me. Though it sounds like you've got your own adrenaline junkie moves going on."

"That trick you pulled on my shares."

"When I tripled them?"

"I need you to do it again."

Silence screamed loudly on the other end.

I whispered, "Quadruple it."

My thoughts carried me to the first time I'd met Richard at Terry's Tavern back at Harvard. He'd looked so young, so intense, nursing his Corona in that private leather seated enclave. His broodiness attracted attention and at the same time kept away those threatened by his looks and obvious wealth.

I wished I could go back to those days at Harvard and start over.

Maybe even choose business instead...

I remembered Richard's nose stuck in Geoffrey Chaucer's *The House of Fame*, while he took bites out of a burger...

I'd approached him. "Mind if I join you?"

"Actually I do." He'd raised his book. "I'm at a good part."

"Great book. It's about truth."

"I don't suck dick."

"Charming, Mr. Sheppard." I'd eased in and sat opposite.

"Can I help you with something?"

"I'm here to guide you to a place where you can safely spank your very own submissive and not get thrown out of Harvard."

He pushed his plate aside and wiped his hands on the napkin.

"Your lover is friends with my ex," I told him.

"Excuse me?"

"Things went a little awry the other night with Megan, apparently."

"This is kind of private."

The waiter hurried over to our table since the bar was empty. Only a few locals sipping beer here and there. The young man was like so many other students who were also closing in on their finals. Those dark circles under his eyes were a result of burning the midnight oil.

I pointed to Richard's burger. "Another one of those, please."

Richard's back straightened defensively.

"A glass of red, perhaps." Though on pursuing the wine list, I changed my mind. "Actually, make that champagne."

"With a burger?" Richard scoffed.

I'd handed the waiter the wine menu back. "Extra chilled."

Richard looked over at him. "Another Corona."

"Sure." Our waiter headed off.

"Shouldn't that be biology?" I gestured to Richard's book.

"You seem to know an awful lot about me."

"It's a small place."

"Bullshit. Listen, pretty boy, I've already told your other cult members I don't do frat houses."

"Sounds like you're a popular man."

"Did Megan send you to talk to me?"

I raised a brow. "No, but she did share you're into kink."

"You her brother?"

"No. I'm here as your friend." I beamed at him, amused.

He shook his head, amused by his own bad boy front and obviously taken by my ability to disarm with a smile.

"I'm offering you the chance of a lifetime, Sheppard," I said. "I'm inviting you to D'envoûtement."

"Enthrall?"

I smiled at his translation.

His gaze swept the bar. "Does that place really exist?"

"It does."

"Catch?"

"You end it with Megan."

"Why?"

"She can't give you what you want and both of you are going to get hurt."

"I like her."

"Tell her you're over."

"You want her?"

I gave him the glare his question deserved.

"All I did was spank her," he said.

"Did she deserve it?"

His frown deepened.

"I'm going to give you your very own submissive," I said. "One who knows how to please a master and will enter subspace

when you spank her. Not cry like Megan did because she's not into your kink."

"She cried?"

"Yes."

"Now I feel like a shit." He took a swig of beer. "She told me she liked it."

"Girls lie."

"How much?"

"For membership?" I shook my head. "All we ask is that you spoil your sub. You keep your mouth shut. You answer to me."

"Sounds like it's your club?"

Our waiter placed that tall glass of champagne in front of me and I watched him walk away. "Am I drinking to our new member?"

"Who the fuck are you?"

"Cameron Cole."

"Of Cole Tea?"

"Yes."

"Heard you're not studying business? Bet that's a disappointment to your dad."

"Neither are you." I took a sip of champagne.

"Looks like we have something in common."

"Same predilection. I can help you."

"Why?"

"It's what I do."

"What? Seek out perverted bastards and offer them a safe place to practice their fucked-up fuckery?"

"Actually I was referring to your squeamishness in the lab. You're failing your first semester because you couldn't handle dissecting Mr. Pukesville." The name he'd given his cadaver. He didn't need to know how I knew that.

Richard visibly paled.

"I can help you with that too," I said.

His gaze narrowed. "You can shove both offers right up your ass."

I slid the card with D'envoûtement's address across the table. "Tomorrow. Eight sharp. Black tie."

I left him staring down at the card.

"Cole, you don't want your burger?" he called after me.

I turned and looked back at him. "I ordered it for Megan."
He'd looked aghast.

Over the years, it wouldn't be the last time Richard had stared at me like that. Richard Booth Sheppard, one of the most incredible friends I'd ever had.

"Cameron?" His voice brought me back to the present.

The scent of Balik salmon, caviar, and coffee lingered, along with the staleness of a meeting long over.

From behind the glass, I could see Dad talking to one of his secretaries. His gaze met mine and he gave a thin smile with a sharp nod of reassurance.

He wanted me to know he was okay.

Inside he was dying.

I cursed Shay for interrupting, believing that perhaps, just perhaps, I could have turned them around. I really thought I had them. Their expressions and body language had proved their conflict.

Had some of them been willing to throw themselves on their swords and ride out the blackmail? Stay loyal?

"Richard," I said. "Do your thing."

"Maybe you need a more experienced broker?"

"You're the best there is."

"I don't know, Cam."

"No regrets."

"Promise."

"Of course."

The line wavered in and out and his voice broke up.

"Richard, are you there?"

"As soon as I get home I'll get on it."

"Pull over and buy from your phone."

"…don't like the sound of this, Cole. You sound a little…"

Uncertain was the word he was reaching for.

I drew back on the doubt in my tone. "Make this happen."

"You're really putting this kind of pressure on me?"

"I'm carrying this, Richard."

"Don't blame me if this goes tits up."

"If you pull this off—"

"It's impossible. You do realize that?"

"What one man can do another can do."

I'd heard that somewhere and truly believed it.

"What do I get out of it?" he said.

"Other than the generous commission?"

"Yeah?"

"Name it. Anything."

"For reals, player?"

He made me smile, and God I needed that right now. "You have my word."

"Mia," he said. "I want her back. If I pull this off, she's mine."

A chill washed over me.

"There's this shiny new stock coming out of Silicon Valley," he continued as though he'd not just threatened to cut out my heart. "An Asian company called Destiny-Horizon. It's skyrocketing. Want me to go for it?"

I spun round and faced the window.

"So we have a deal, Cameron?"

My mouth dry. "Richard."

The call dropped.

The line went dead.

I redialed and it went to voicemail.

Staring at my phone, I reran over our conversation, feeling as though I'd not been present. It was a surreal out of body experience.

What the fuck had just happened?

I stared out at the panoramic view and it made me feel so small, so useless.

Out of control.

Men had worked tirelessly building those skyscrapers, waterways, and bridges in a true testimony of what we were capable of—the confidence to create breathtaking monuments, each brick a landmark of determination never to give up.

A statement of unyielding power.

All I had to do was remember to breathe.

Do what had to be done.

CHAPTER 19

THE ELEVATOR ASCENDED.

A smooth ride toward the penthouse.

I'd moved Mia and I to my parent's Manhattan Tempest Tower, right up there on the 98th story. We needed to find a place with no distractions and take advantage of this privacy.

My sleepless nights might end in a place with no memories.

I was only half aware of the view of Central Park. The midmorning sun reflected off the glass, causing me to squint and shield my eyes. These luxury suites were just another piece of real estate my parents owned.

Their penthouse was lavishly decorated by my mother's designer, and I cringed at the impending blast of color that was imminent. Leaning on the wall to support this sudden weakness, fatigue soaked into my bones and drenched my thoughts with futility.

The door flung open and Mia leaped onto me, wrapping her legs around my waist and hugging me. Her joy provided a stark contrast to my stunned state.

She slipped from me and I felt the loss of her.

She searched my face. "You did it!"

I cupped her cheeks and kissed her passionately, despite this ache making me want to push her away. Reluctant to tell her, I tried to find the words to let her down gently. This battle had been just as much hers.

"I went exploring," she said. "There's this nice little deli one block away. I bought lunch for everyone."

"Thank you," I said. "We won't be needing it now."

"But Henry's on his way over? And Shay? Why don't you get some sleep before they get here? You look exhausted."

"They're not coming."

Her smile faded.

I took her by the hand and guided her farther in. "Mia."

"Cameron, what happened?"

"Everyone we visited yesterday rescinded their vote."

"But that doesn't make any sense."

I moved away, hating myself for allowing this to go so wrong, for failing my dad, failing everyone.

"Cameron?"

"Someone got to them."

"The men behind the buyout?"

"Pure and simple blackmail."

"Go to the police."

"It doesn't work like that."

Her eyes watered. "Your dad's lawyers then."

"An investigation would end the same. Their privacy shattered. Then they'd willingly throw us to the wolves. It's lose, lose."

"There must be something you can do?"

"We've run out of time."

"No, I refuse to believe that. Not after everything you did?"

I shrugged, not wanting her to see me like this. "I have to make some calls."

"What can I do?"

I shook my head, trying to clear my thoughts.

Striding away, I headed into the study, needing to put distance between us.

The morning sun burst like shards of fierce orange through the window, and I blinked against the assault and strolled over to close the blinds.

Making my way back toward the desk, I felt useless and stood there merely staring at the wall.

Too tired to sleep. To eat. Do anything of value.

Chaos.

This inner violence found its freedom.

There came a sense of movement, yet at the same time standing still.

"Cameron?" Mia lingered in the doorway. "What did you do?"

"It was right there," I said. "We had them."

"Surely there's something you can do?"

Had I just promised to return her to Richard? I couldn't remember, couldn't think straight. The thought of losing her was impossible to contemplate.

Was this the bitter taste of insanity?

I turned and I too stared in horror—

The contents of the desk were now strewn on the floor. Papers, files, pens, and even the computer was tipped over on the carpet. I had a vague memory of being responsible.

Seconds passed with stubbornness.

The last time I'd wrecked a room like this, it had been Richard's dungeon in London when I'd realized I couldn't have Mia. I'd allowed rage to own me as I'd ripped the place apart and tipped over that Saint Andrew's Cross. It had taken two men to right it after the fact—proof of super human strength when consumed with torment, with gut wrenching heartache.

Cole Tea, an empire I was never destined to save.

It had always been Henry's. His to master whenever he chose. Had some part of me reasoned with this? The second born destined for the shadows.

The rush of business had absorbed me these last few days, having resigned to my destiny, the promise of new challenges. An adrenaline ride like no other.

I was my father's son.

"You're going to get some sleep." Mia pulled me out of there, down the hallway, and into the bedroom.

Her hands were on me, removing my coat, jacket, shirt, stripping me naked, and I stood there letting this out of body experience ease my exhaustion.

My gaze fell on the contract.

Mia caught me looking at it, headed over, and grabbed it off the table.

She threw it out the room. "It's probably not even in there." She shut the door and returned to my side.

Mia knelt before me. "Master, I'm going to help you relax."

My head fell back as she took my cock into her mouth, her tongue lapping my length. My eyelids grew heavy with need and my gaze drifted to the door.

That document out there supposedly held the answer. Again, I ran over those endless words of endless assertions, with citations to prove their authority and quantify their reasoning. Where was that one line that would shore up the weakness buried somewhere in those endless pages.

A yell of frustration threatened to tear from me.

My gaze lowered to take in the stunning beauty at my feet suckling, giving me what I needed, bringing me closer to clarity.

She stared up at me. "We're going to sleep together tonight."

Those words had become our private mantra of affection.

I wished that were possible.

...give her back?

Let her go.

I leaned unsteadily.

My thoughts trailed behind the illogical.

A company's future no longer hanging in the balance.

It really was over.

Mia rose to her feet and stepped back. "What did you just say?"

"Didn't say anything."

"Yes, you did." She looked stunned. "You just said something about returning me to Richard."

Blinking, I tried to read her.

Yes, I'd thought those words, but had I really spoken that threat out loud? Was I this tired?

"He mentioned it," I whispered.

"You don't know what I went through," she snapped. "I fell in love with Richard because you wanted me to. You orchestrated it. You made it happen. Then he gave me to you. Thrust me into your arms and I fell hard for you, Cameron. You became my reason to live. When you gave me back to him, I was drowning. You couldn't see it—"

"I did—"

"All I thought of was you."

"Everything's changed."

Our lives turned upside down.

She hugged herself. "What did you tell him?"

"I delayed my answer."

The call had dropped. The only reason. Blackmail had never been my thing.

Mia stepped back. "I'm happy you've lost it all."

"Well that's enlightening."

"Now you know without any doubt I didn't care for this." Her hand swept around us. "I love you, Cameron. I love being in your presence, and I love everyone knowing you and I are in love. I'm proud to be your woman."

I reached for my shirt and pulled it on. "You're happy I failed?"

"You now know without a doubt I love you."

"You make me lose control, Mia." I shook my head. "This is not good."

"No, I'm the only certainty you have, Cameron. I yearn for your control. Crave it. I'm the yang to your yin."

"Other way round."

"What?"

"Male is yin, female yang."

"Thank you for correcting me," she snapped.

"I'm used to it."

"Fuck you."

"Technically male's fuck females."

"Are you being purposefully obtuse?" she said. "I know you're hurting and my heart aches for you but—"

"Big word for you."

"You arrogant ass."

I arched a brow. "I'm merely proving you're the lesser species."

"Someone's going to want sex later. That someone will not be getting any."

"You'll get over it."

"I meant you."

I took a step closer. "This is all very idiotic."

"Not as idiotic as telling me you're considering giving me back to a man I don't love. Not like that anyway."

"So you admit you still love him?"

"I'm not a piece of property to be handed around."

"Welcome to my world."

"Cameron, I love you. And nothing you say or do is going to change that."

"As soon as we get back to L.A., I'm going to lock you in that cage."

"And I'm going to thrive in it," she snapped. "Because knowing you are going to rescue me from it will be what keeps me alive."

I flew at her, lifting her up and flinging her on the bed, and she reached for me.

Tugging her dress up and over her, I was greeted by a smile when her face reappeared on the other side.

A fucking smile.

God, how I loved her.

I flung her dress on the floor and her bra and panties soon joined her dress.

I shrugged out of my shirt. "Did you honestly believe I'd ever give you up?"

"You considered it?"

"No, Mia. The call dropped before I could tell Richard that was ridiculous." I pinned her arms above her head. "You doubting me has its consequences."

"What does that mean?"

"You'll apologize"

"I will not."

"What was that about a sex ban?"

She suppressed a smile. "Have no idea what you're talking about."

"You're easily swayed, Ms. Lauren." I pressed my cock against her sex.

Mia opened her legs farther and rocked against me. "You're also the master of persuasion, Dr. Cole."

"I've lost everything, yet you make me feel like I've won."

"You need to sleep."

"Want me to stop?"

"No, I just feel selfish right now." Her head fell back, her long moan making me harder.

Tangled together, our kiss deep and passionate, our tongues

intertwined, our fight was not for supremacy but to prove to each other how deep our love went, as though words failed us. The only truth was this, my mouth taking hers in a desperate fucking of souls.

Inside her now, I was unable to fathom how I'd not taken her like this, hard and fast, when I'd first stepped out of the elevator. This was the best way to find my center again.

Mia, where truth and beauty always waited for me.

"I was fighting for us, Mia, for our future."

"You did everything you could, Cameron. You've given it your all."

"Wasn't enough."

"We have each other," she whispered.

Rocking into her, her tight and demanding sex caused my mind to splinter into a vortex of nothingness and I came hard. My warmth filled her, and my thoughts were gone, lost in this sea of pleasure.

I rose up and stared down at her.

She smiled. "You needed that."

I shook my head, trying to rid myself of this fatigue.

I'd never come before a woman before. Ever. I was losing my edge.

Rising off Mia, I left the bed and went in search of my tie, bringing it back and tying her wrists together. I secured her to the headboard with the other end.

"Bring your legs up," I said.

She obeyed, blinking with curiosity, watching.

Mia, my only hope of ever forgiving myself.

Sitting up beside her, I stroked her sex, resting a fingertip there now, circling slowly, feeling it swell. Her thighs trembled.

On and on I caressed, patiently allowing her climax to ascend and comforted by seeing her rise. She rose ever more until she reached that pinnacle. I continued on, sustaining Mia there until her jaw became slack, her body quivered, and her endless orgasm seduced her.

Pride swelled in me at seeing proof I'd marked her as my own with my seed, fused with this gratification at how she responded to my touch. Her cries of bliss filled the room.

That all-consuming tension of titillation burned between her thighs, concentrated in her core, making her nipples hard and erect. Shards of morning light danced over her complexion. I was at a perfect vantage point to admire the curves of a woman, watch her writhe, see her beholden to me.

With my other hand, I lowered her pelvis back down when she raised her hips, again demanding she surrender to the intensity.

This was the very same reward and punishment I'd bestowed when I'd released her from Chrysalis's dungeon. Those days and night of her confinement seemed like light years away now. Those profound hours spent together working through her darkest memories and freeing her from the emotional chains that had bound her.

In my world, our self-inflicted bondage with chains, cuffs, and ropes was never about containment, but freedom, a letting go.

An allowing.

Finding freedom through another and proving without a doubt we are not islands of being, but needful of each other.

And God how I needed her.

Her deep gasps for air filled the room. Her orgasm stole her breath.

I slid beneath her with her back to my front and I glided into her again. Her wrists still bound together ensured her powerlessness.

"I don't think I can go again," she said in a rush.

I reached around for her breasts, tweaking her nipples. "When is fucking finished, Ms. Lauren?"

"Oh, God."

"Answer me."

"When you say it is, sir."

"Good girl."

Raising my hips, thrusting into her, my one hand played with her nipples. I took my time on one and then the other. My other fingertips trailed between her legs, flicking her clit expertly. My cock drove into her and her slickness aided my fierce pounding. This heat of pleasure rose and burned through my core.

Her head rested in the crook of my neck, and her small gasps were endearing. My hand delighting in sliding over her wetness, not caring about the noise of a squeaking bed, or her screaming as she came...

Despite all of it—

Empires falling, enemies taking aim and sealing our fate—Mia outshone all those falsehoods, those desperate men who'd failed to learn what it was to truly love. To find peace in the center of a storm.

We came together and collapsed together, our body's spotted in perspiration and heated from all this tussling, our fucking the purist form of any bondage.

My body yearned for sleep but didn't find it. I was too tired to let go.

My only comfort was Mia laying her head on my chest, her leg flung over me, breathing softly as she slipped into sleep. I didn't move for fear of waking her. Instead I stared up at the ceiling, running through the last few days and re-living them until I'd improved on my strategy and fooled myself I'd won out.

I'd been working in the dark, moving forward in an unfamiliar world, and unlike the science based career I'd chosen, business was full of trap doors and secrets and misdirection.

"What did you say earlier?" I whispered.

"About your cage."

I grinned. "The contract—" I eased away from her and climbed out of bed and it felt wrong to leave her side.

I padded out to retrieve the document.

When I came back, Mia was stretching languidly, showing a hint of nipple.

The brilliance of a woman.

I slammed the contract on the side table. "Mia, you're a fucking genius."

She sat up. "Must be rubbing off, Dr. Cole."

I rested my hand on the contract. "It was never in here."

CHAPTER 20

THE COMPUTER STILL worked.

Which was a small miracle. After rescuing it from the floor, I plugged it back in and fired it up.

Having only slipped on my pants, too excited to dress, I felt the chill of this place. Mia was brewing coffee and the delicious aroma filled my nostrils.

A rush of adrenaline drove me on as I clicked through the emails of my father's late attorney, Dan Stork. I used the keyboard's control and F-key to search for keywords in each one to speed up the process.

My heart thundered.

I found it.

The world around me disappeared as the last remnants of my focus took in the small print.

The members of the board's days were numbered.

Dan Stork had placed a link to an addendum within the contract, thus leaving out the jargon that defined the terms of the board. He'd sent the details via email and masterfully camouflaged it from every member. These men received hundreds of emails a day and therefore left their assistants to troll through the minutia.

Everyone had missed the fine print tucked in-between the minutes taken during a meeting they'd attended, and thus thought nothing of signing what they had already read. They'd signed the email electronically, sealing their fate.

I re-read Dan's legal spiel, cunningly designed to bore the reader and throw them off the scent of what they were actually signing:

Should sole means of operational status be obtained by any single member of the board, all members will be held accountable for such action. The resulting consequence shall be immediate and resolute dissolution of their heretofore granted right to function and proceed as a member of said board.

Stork had hidden the content between the number of charity functions planned out for the year. My dad had always told us to read the small print, and even he hadn't taken his own advice. Luckily for Dad, Stork had been his loyal attorney and friend, and even from the grave he'd proven that.

Stork had inserted an ingenious defensive tactic. A paradox of power. The definitive poison pill. One that gave Dad the power to swing the axe or choose leniency.

And they'd signed off on it. I forwarded what I'd found in an email to Dad, and then left a voicemail for his assistant to schedule another meeting.

This document had bought us time.

Half in a daze, I slid my mouse over to the Dow and then went in search of the current state of my stock.

It didn't make any sense.

My personal shares were decimated.

"Destiny-Horizon. It's skyrocketing," Richard had told me.

But the numbers reflected the shares had taken a hit and were now worthless.

I rose to my feet—

Reaching for the mouse again, I refreshed the screen.

Staggering back—

Disbelief.

My legs went weak, and my gait was unsteady as I knocked into the chair and tipped it over.

I barely made it to the restroom. There, I leaned over the sink and retched into it. Bile rose as my stomach twisted and convulsed.

The dreadful taste.

My reflection in the mirror revealed a man who'd pushed

himself to the edge and beyond. Dark circles wreathed beneath my eyes and my face was pallid.

My money was gone. All of it. The funds once entrusted to me by my father, and earned with pride over generations who'd gone before me, was no more.

I rinsed out my mouth with shaking hands, dizzy from the realization everything had come crashing down. What had gone wrong? I'd moved the chess pieces, masterminding the plan that had always been destined to implode.

The architect of my own downfall.

Unsteadily, I walked back into the office and found my phone. My fingers struggled to still long enough to scroll for his number.

"Cole?" answered Richard. "'Bout time. Where are you?"

"Tempest Tower," I said weakly. "My dad's signing over the company."

"What? Why?"

I leaned on the back of a chair for support.

"Cameron, are you okay?"

"Are you enjoying this?"

"What the fuck? Is Mia there? Put her on."

"Is this about her?" My voice sounded foreign, forced.

"I knew you'd never give her back."

"I can't breathe without her." My back hit the wall and I slid down it, clutching the phone to my ear. "Did you do this on purpose?" Even as I spoke those words, I didn't believe them, couldn't comprehend I'd not seen this coming.

Blinded by love, exhaustion, the madness of pride. The raw truth that love took down kingdoms. I'd always known that.

I'd done the unspeakable to my best friend and my arrogance had made me believe there'd be no consequences.

Can't think straight. I struggled to hold a thought.

"I just hope you're willing to live with the consequences," said Richard. "Don't blame me when your life is turned upside down."

I threw my phone across the room and it bounced off the table, the screen shattering.

I still couldn't hate him, though it was easy to curse myself for giving him the power to destroy me. The one man who I'd let get close and the last person I'd believed could hurt me.

No air in here.

The lack of oxygen grew all-consuming as I tried to remember what it was to breathe.

What day? What time? What place was this?

A blur of movement.

Mia hurried in and she'd pulled on one of my shirts. She waved her cell in the air. "Richard's trying to call you." She looked around. "Where's yours?"

"Hang up."

"He says it's important."

"Richard's wallowing in my downfall."

"He wouldn't do that." She knelt before me and pushed her phone at me. "He's on the line."

I grabbed her phone and threw it across the room and it bounced off the carpet and landed under the table.

"Cameron?" She ran after it and went on all fours to retrieve it, dragging it out and pressing it to her ear. "Hello? Please tell Cameron to get some sleep. He's exhausted. Richard, please, he listens to you."

I had listened to him, trusted him.

A surge of anger washed over me and I pushed myself to my feet, gesturing for the phone.

Mia handed it to me.

"Richard?" I said.

"When was the last time you got any sleep?" he said.

"It was never about the money," I snapped. "It was about a greater purpose. And if this is your way of getting me to realize how much I love Mia, well bravo, Richard Booth Sheppard. She's worth more to me than anyone will ever know. I never meant to hurt you. I've told you that a thousand times. I've begged for your forgiveness. Know this—I will not give her up. Ever."

More empires could fall for all I cared.

Mia would always be mine.

Richard scoffed. "Yeah, I could hear it in your voice when I asked for her back."

I held the phone away from my ear and glared at it.

Mia took the phone from me and punched the speaker and held it between us.

"Cameron," Richard's voice filled the room. "Check your shares."

"I did."

Asshole.

"You think we went with Destiny-Horizon?"

I was literally seeing black spots.

The room became a blur.

"God, I know you so well," he said. "Those looked like crap in the end. We went with Phoenix-Rise. You did give me free rein after all. They just went public—"

"You didn't lose my money?"

"Well that explains your pissy mood."

"Richard?"

"I just made a shitload of commission, thanks to you. We went through Charlie's. Thought it best to buy under your charity name and that way no one would become suspicious that Cameron Cole...are you still there?"

"Richard." His name wouldn't come out. My lips failed to form words and my mind reeled.

"We're still here," said Mia.

"Cam," said Richard. "I quadrupled it."

Breathing no longer was necessary, apparently.

He laughed. "I'm assuming you want me to buy every Cole Tea and Tempest Coffee share I can get my hands on and add it to your portfolio?"

I nodded.

Mia leaned in. "Cameron says 'yes please.'" She beamed at me.

The sound of Richard clicking away filtered through the phone. Winston barked in the background, and Richard told Winston to stop barking.

A lifetime came and went.

A series of memories unfolded and all of them led to this moment.

"That's the only good thing about a rumor of a hostile takeover," said Richard. "People dump their shares."

"What does that mean?" whispered Mia.

"Boom bitches!" shouted Richard.

My heart thundered. "Speak to me."

"You just became the proud owner of Cole Tea. Well, 90% anyway. Not bad for a day's work."

I stared at the phone as though it was the only thing that would save me.

Time sped up. Slowed down. Realization dawned.

"Richard, you're a genius," shouted Mia, jumping up and down.

"Well, we know that." He laughed.

"I have to get back to the tower." I ran out of the office, through the sitting room, and headed for the door.

"Cameron!" Mia ran after me. "Your clothes."

I ran back to her. "Phone." I took it from her. "Richard?"

"Still here."

Mia handed me a sock and I hopped into it with one hand and held the phone with the other. "Richard! Thank you."

"What are you waiting for?" he said. "Go."

CHAPTER 21

RUSH HOUR.

A ridiculously bad time to choose to save an empire.

Outside on the curb with my phone pressed to my ear, I tried to hail a cab while I scanned the chaos around me.

My dad was minutes away from signing over Cole Tea and he wasn't answering his phone. His assistant wasn't answering his either. No one was. Because everyone was probably in the conference room about to witness the dark deed.

Traffic was stationary. Horns blasted. The hustle and bustle of New York surrounded me. Pedestrian's made their way to work and tourists were trickling onto the streets ready to explore.

The futility of frustration. I'd never get there.

I took off, sprinting faster than I ever had, and something told me I was besting my five minute mile.

Passing shops and buildings, I weaved my way through.

Richard had pulled off a miracle. He'd quietly purchased enough stock known as a creeping tender offer to change the face of Cole Tea, and no matter how the board resisted we had full power to deliver the death stroke. Prescribe that poison pill to the men who'd betrayed us.

I crashed through the revolving door and my coat caught. I twisted out of it, leaving it behind and staggering forward, almost tripping as I bolted toward the elevator.

A guard lunged toward me.

"It's Dr. Cole," another shouted, and the guard stood down.

Right on cue, the elevator doors parted and I flew in and punched the button for top floor.

Rising fast, I took this advantage to catch my breath and willed it to go faster. My hands rested on my knees as I sucked in gulps of air, readying for the next sprint to the conference room.

Out and along—

Not caring who I startled, I flew by cubicles and offices. The conference room was tucked all the way in the back.

Staff look defeated as I flew by them. Shell-shocked.

Through the glass, I saw Dad at the head of the table and Henry sat by his side. Paul, Dad's assistant, looked just as devastated. The young man had been crying.

This was to be a private affair, apparently.

At the end of the corridor, as though waiting to feast on what remained, stood the members of the board, and they turned to greet me.

I ignored them—

Bursting in, turning sharply, I slammed the door behind me.

Dad's frown deepened as though my entering was an assault on his senses. His white knuckled grip on the pen faltered.

Henry looked just as drawn and tired, but pushed himself to his feet to greet me.

"Tell me you didn't sign it," I said breathlessly, making way toward them.

"Cameron, it's over," said Dad. His pen met the paper, and a blotch of ink formed as he began to scrawl his signature.

I reached over and snapped the pen out of his hand.

"Paul," I said. "Frost the glass. Now, please."

He hurried over and shielded us from the prying eyes of those shark infested corridors.

Dad's glare met my smiling eyes. "What's going on?"

"Cam, we're out of time," said Henry, his voice hoarse.

"You don't need to sign it, Dad." I said.

His stare swept over the contact.

I gestured to Paul. "Please, give us some privacy."

With a nod, Dad gave Paul permission to leave.

I threw them both a big smile. "We're going to draw up a new contract."

"How?" said Henry.

"We own 90% of Cole Tea," I said, hardly believing it. "The shares hit the market and we bought them up."

Dad rose from his chair. "With what?"

"All our money's tied up," said Henry.

I moved closer to them. "Richard pulled a few tricks on the stock market with my portfolio—"

"Legally?" snapped Henry.

"Of course," I said. "He made us enough money to go ahead and purchase what we need to own the majority." I arched a brow. "And some."

"We're talking billions?" said Dad.

His doubt hit hard.

These seconds of silence served their purpose for thoughts to settle and minds to comprehend what had looked impossible.

Dad slumped back into his chair.

Henry stared at me. "You mean you now own Cole Tea?"

"On paper, but it's our money, right?"

"This is…" Dad pushed the contract away.

"A good thing." My gaze rested on the frosted glass—a symbol of my father's thoughts. "Cole Tea is still in the family." This adrenaline threatened never to wear off.

"You did it," Dad said, braving to believe.

"Henry?" I said.

His face lit up with a smile and he flung himself toward me, wrapping his arms around me in a hug.

CHAPTER 22

I FOUND HENRY in Dad's office.

Instead of sitting on that lengthy sofa, or in either one of those leather chairs, he'd chosen the floor and leaned against the back wall.

"You're missing Dad wearing a party hat," I said.

"Now that I have to see."

"What are you doing in here?"

"Admiring the view."

"An interesting choice of perspective."

"I believed it was over." He gestured to Dad's office chair. "I was devastated for him, but I had this sense of…"

"What?"

"Freedom."

"We're all been under a tremendous pressure," I said. "We need a good meal and sleep—"

"I started fantasizing about owning a football team," he said. "Spending my days touring the world, concentrating on our charities with the money we had left."

"And you still can."

He held my stare.

"Henry, we made it. We won."

"No, Cameron, you won. You pulled this off. While the rest of us were floundering, you kept fighting. You can't see it."

"See what?"

"You were always destined for this."

"No, Henry." My heart rate took off and I ran through my options. "I'll be by your side—"

"You are Cole Tea, Cameron."

"Don't do this, Henry. Not now. Now's the time to celebrate."

"There's no joy in any of it for me. I had to stop myself from yawning during those board meetings. They went on and on and on. All this business jargon that I really have no interest in. Hate those bastards for betraying us. Gone was the camaraderie I'm used to, the loyalty."

"Stork was loyal. He secured a poison pill for the board. They all signed a contract that ensures they're gone."

"Serves them right." Henry looked at me. "I can't wait to see you deliver that news."

"I'll let Dad do the honors."

"Someone got to them."

"We'll find out who."

"He was seconds from signing it. You might want to work on your timing."

"I topped my five minute mile."

"You ran from the suite?"

"Almost broke my neck."

We laughed.

Henry pushed himself to his feet. "Come on. Let's go find Dad and tell him our news."

I rose. "Don't do this. You need time to think this through."

He scrunched up his nose. "I have a feeling you'll vastly improve on the décor."

"Henry, this is your office now."

"What do you see when you look around?"

"Opportunity."

"A cell."

"We'll get you another. A better view."

He lowered his chin as he looked at me.

I valued what Henry wanted above all things, and after my own struggle with this, the memory of it dragged not far behind. I'd never put him through this kind of conflict. He'd already sacrificed enough.

We both made our way back to the conference room where we

found Dad, alone and staring out at the view.

As though Dad had always suspected it, he allowed Henry to gracefully back out, and as I watched my older brother resign his future over to me, there came a wave of guilt, alongside relief that finally I felt ready.

Henry left.

His expression seemed calmer.

Through the glass, I saw Mia greet him. Her comforting smile and her wave let me know she'd watch over him.

Turning to face the window, shoulder to shoulder with my father, both of us took in the awe-inspiring vista of New York's skyline.

Dad wrapped an arm around me.

CHAPTER 23

HENRY SAT ON the edge of the marble fountain, breaking off pieces of bread and feeding it to the swans. Their necks stretched out, eager for more.

I'd never known a time when we'd not had swans.

The lake twinkled in the moonlight.

We were both dressed in black tie, ready for dinner and itching for an end to all this formality. This etiquette was overly constricting.

For the first time since I'd landed in New York, a calmness descended on me as though only now I realized what we'd pulled off. The Cole name was destined to rule the tea market for decades to come.

I sat beside Henry. "I like it out here."

"Me too."

"It's peaceful."

He pointed to the swans. "Something tells me you and Mia are going to be like this pair here."

"I hope so."

He threw out another piece. "I've never seen you so happy, Cam. She's your true north."

"She's been my rock through all this."

"And you've been mine."

"Please change your mind, Henry."

He took a deep sigh. "Trust me, I've given it the thought it deserves."

"And?"

"I watched you. The way your blood boiled in the boardroom, the respect you commanded because you refused to back down." He balled a fist in passion. "I've never seen you so driven about anything." His gaze lowered. "Other than Mia, of course."

"I'm giving up everything. My world is upside down."

"Doubt?"

"Cautiously proceeding."

"Well you've made Mom happy. I heard her singing in the study. She was wearing overalls and painting the wall, hiding our evidence. I mean, fuck, talk about the most remarkable intervention I've ever seen."

I threw my head back in a laugh.

"You think I'm joking," he said.

"Can't imagine it."

"Trust me, I've tried to push that vision out of my mind."

I pointed to the swans. "Do they have names?"

"Willow's probably given them some. They remind me of you. Always so calm on the surface but underneath so much going on."

"Not sure that's a good thing."

"You keep your cool, Cam. That's why you're perfect at the helm."

"Henry, you're more than capable."

"Too late now. Your name's on the office supplies." He winked at me.

"I'm not letting you off the hook that easily."

"We both know that's no way to run an empire."

"Still."

"Did you get some sleep?"

"Power nap."

He rolled his eyes. "Which means you can't keep your hands off each other."

"She's captivated me. What can I tell you."

"Maybe I'll be calling her sister, soon?"

I beamed at him. "I suppose we should get ready for dinner."

"Thank you, Cam."

"What for?"

"Helping Dad see we're all making the right decision."

"You were always my hero. You know that, don't you? Always braver. Faster. Smarter, funnier, and you always got the girls."

He frowned at me. "That was you, Cam."

"No, you thrived at boarding school. You won medal after medal."

"Again, that was you."

"I didn't win a thing."

"Seriously?"

"Nope."

"The word loser comes to mind."

I knocked into him.

He turned to face me. "Didn't you win that chess game against that ass Davis? Wasn't he a senior? You won in five moves?"

"Doesn't count."

"Of course it counts."

"I suffered the consequences for that one."

"How do you mean?"

"Davis didn't like to lose."

"I wished you'd told me. I'd have killed the bastard."

"Which was why I didn't tell you."

He looked horrified.

"I got my own back," I said.

"Do I even want to know?"

"No. Your opinion of me would be changed forever."

"Talking of scandals…"

"I know."

"Do you think you can give it up?"

"I'm heading back to L.A. first thing tomorrow to begin the process of handing over the clinic."

"I meant Chrysalis."

Of course he did, and it pained me to think of closing that door after I'd so carefully constructed this sanctuary for likeminded people who dared to ignore the confines of society and explore the dark arts in all their glory.

The lifeblood of Enthrall and Chrysalis ran through my veins, and soon I'd be faced with the inevitable. My enemies could not be given any ammunition to destroy me and my past had to be carefully orchestrated, wiped clean—my public persona redesigned to fit the corporate world.

I'd be giving up so much, but the promise of what this city had to offer, and what I knew I could do for our company, was an unexplored yearning.

Henry pointed to a swan. "That one just gave you the stink eye."

"I think he was giving it to you."

"He's a she."

"How can you tell?"

"Seriously?"

I couldn't remember laughing like this in a long time. My gaze turned toward the house and I needed to go find Mia, needed to tell her how much she meant to me and thank her for standing by me during all this.

"We'll talk every day Henry. Promise?"

"That won't get tedious at all."

"I'm serious."

"Go on then. Go find your girl."

I pushed myself to my feet.

He stood too and opened his arms. I fell into his embrace.

Our bond had transcended the years and had endured too much torment. But we were still standing, still moving forward, and our future felt safer than ever before.

I headed off to find Mia.

First I stopped off at the office safe where I retrieved that flat square velvet box.

After exchanging texts, I found her hiding out in the library. She'd dressed for dinner in a black halter dress and she'd slipped into delicate heels. Her hair was neatly tied back to subdue her locks, pulling back on her feisty style.

Mia sat in a corner chair near the fire.

She peered up from her book.

"What are you reading?" I neared her.

She raised it. "Your mom gave it to me. It's about the museums and galleries here. I think she's trying to make me feel at home."

Now that was progress.

"What's that?" she said excitedly, staring at the box.

I glanced down at it. "A box."

"A collar?"

"Perhaps."

Her cheeks flushed brightly.

I hid it behind my back.

She laughed at that.

"Ready to fly out tonight?" I said.

"All packed. How's Henry?"

"Doing great, considering the pressure we put him under." I shook my head. "I put him under."

"You can't blame yourself."

"It's all such bad timing. Had this happened a few years down the line…"

"Your father told him the door's always open."

I sat on the arm of her chair and peered down at the book. "The Museum of Natural History is worth checking out. We'll go."

"I'm excited."

"We'll fly Bailey and Tara out to visit."

"I'd love that."

"Good."

"Cameron, can I ask you something?"

"Anything. You know that."

"Everything happened so fast. We never got to talk about it."

"It?"

"What went wrong with you and Zie? It's just that you both seemed so happy once."

I gave a nod. "It became complicated."

Mia stared down at the page. "What if I make the same mistake as her?"

"You won't."

"I need to know why you both didn't work out."

Taking a steadying breath, I stared down at her. Mia reached for my hand and gave it a comforting squeeze.

"One evening, late at work, I became sick," I said. "Nothing serious. Just the flu. But I felt like hell and decided to call it a day. You know, take my own advice. Zie wouldn't have known I was coming home early."

"Did you find her with someone?"

"She wasn't home."

"Where was she?"

"Chrysalis."

"How did you find her there?"

"Her masquerade mask was missing from the closet."

"So you knew?"

"I found her in the Harrington Suite." I dropped my gaze, hoping to conceal how even now it affected me.

Mia's eyes widened. "You saw her with someone?"

"You could say that."

Mia blinked her understanding. "Not just one man?"

"As though I wouldn't find out."

"What'd you do?"

"Called off our engagement. Then banned the doms who'd fucked her."

"How can you go in there again?"

"Scars keep us focused."

"We need to replace that memory, Cameron."

I offered a kind smile. "Have something in mind?"

"As a matter of fact, yes."

"Mia, we're going to have to put Chrysalis behind us."

"Let's make our final visit memorable."

I brushed a stray hair out of her eyes. "Are you suggesting a public fucking, Ms. Lauren?"

Her teeth scraped her lower lip and her gaze rose to meet mine.

"In the Harrington Suite?" I said.

She beamed. "Go out with a bang!"

I brought the box around and opened it. "Then you'll need this."

A flash of sparkling Cartier diamonds lined the choker, catching the light in a brilliant prism—a stunning collection of the finest gems.

Mia leaped from her chair and into my arms.

CHAPTER 24

IT WAS DONE.

Saving the demise of a billion dollar empire had been so much easier than saying goodbye to my patients.

Mia and I had flown back to L.A. three nights ago, and it was with a heavy heart I'd not be staying in the city I'd come to love. But there came an excitement about our future. A new challenge. A destiny that only now I was ready for.

I'd spent the day at my Beverly Hills office finalizing the details.

My last consultation had been with Brian, a gentle comic book artist who lived just off Mulholland. He'd suffered with agoraphobia for years. The very fact he'd made it to my office to say goodbye and meet Laura, his new doctor, proved we'd made progress. Though when I'd delivered the news I was moving to New York, his expression had almost ruined me. He'd been under my protection for years, and of all my patients I'd miss our visits the most.

Laura promised she'd visit him at home too and that seemed to comfort him. I promised to visit Brian when next in town. It was good to see him cope with the news.

With the clinic now closing for the day, I presented Patricia with her goodbye gift—a delicate Rolex watch. She'd been my secretary for years and had always handled my affairs with professionalism. I'd miss her, not least because it was fun to guess her latest hair color, which changed more than the seasons. Today she'd gone for blue.

It was a tearful goodbye, but Patricia soon calmed when I helped secure her new watch to her wrist. She promised to be my eyes and ears at the clinic and contact me should any issue arise. I'd invested too many years into this place to give up caring for it so easily.

I headed back into Laura's office for my final goodbye and to make sure she knew she'd be locking up after I'd sent Patricia home early.

Laura had gone to the bathroom to touch up her makeup. She had a dinner date tonight, and I had a feeling it was with her new lover.

My phone vibrated in my pocket.

"Shay," I said. "Tell me you have good news."

"Actually," he said. "We've found him."

"Where?"

"Adrian's in Germany. Has relatives there. He's laying low."

"What's the next step?"

"We'll talk to him. Make sure he behaves."

"Shay?"

"I know."

"Don't—"

"So, how's the move going?"

"Good."

"I'll see you tonight?"

"Looking forward to it. Shay?"

"Yes."

"Thank you, for everything. I couldn't have done it without you."

"I appreciate that, Cam."

"Assign your staff to Chrysalis," I said. "I want you to enjoy this evening."

"That an order?"

"It is."

I killed the call.

Whatever was going on in Germany right now was out of my control. And I hated that feeling.

The last time I'd been in here, Zie had delivered that skewered news about what she believed was going on at Charlie's. My gaze roamed the table, chairs, and artwork.

That session with Zie and Laura rolled through my brain like the dark memory it was, yet with all this talk of closure and moving on I felt like the one who needed resolution now.

At my feet lay that trash can I'd mused over briefly, and curiosity led me to kneel and rummage through the few papers within. Laura cleaned out her handbag each day and here lay a trail of evidence.

How remarkable that one small piece of paper—a drink receipt from the Pump Lounge in Santa Monica for two margaritas could deliver the truth. It had been there all along, right in front of me, only Zie's presence had thrown me off from seeing it. Being on the defensive, no part of me had thought to come out fighting. I'd merely needed to see her happy again.

And happy Zie was, in her new relationship with her smart and pretty girlfriend.

Laura breezed in with the air of someone carrying the new title of director of the clinic, and I was reassured I'd be handing over the office to such a dedicated professional.

"How are you doing?" she asked.

"Everyone took it well, so there's some reassurance."

"You're making the right decision."

"Thank you, Laura. I feel that way too."

"Mia's okay with moving to New York?"

"She's excited. She's leaving behind her best friends, but I've promised to fly Bailey and Tara out whenever they want."

"That's nice of you."

"Least I can do. Couldn't have done this without her."

"Sure you could."

"She's been my rock."

"Look after her."

"She'll always be my priority. I'm reassured you're our new director, Laura. Please, don't hesitate to call me should anything come up."

"I'm sure I will."

"So dinner tonight?"

She hesitated. "I'm meeting a friend."

I unraveled the receipt.

She stared at it.

The way Laura had stared at Zie, the way she'd touched her knee to comfort her, her blushes when Zie's sexual past was discussed all gave her away.

"How long?" I said.

"Excuse me?"

"How long have you been dating Zie?"

She swallowed hard and blushed. "That's very presumptive."

"She tastes amazing, doesn't she?" I whispered it.

Laura's blush reached her neck. Her carotid pulse subtly quickened and her stance changed as her thoughts carried her all the way to Zie. Perhaps to last night, or this morning. Wherever her thoughts took her it caused her pupils to dilate, her nipples to harden.

I raised the receipt. "Two margaritas. One blended, just how you like it. The other straight..."

She cringed when she realized.

"Well?" I said.

"Please don't tell anyone."

After what I'd put Mia through I was hardly innocent, but Laura didn't need to know that. "Laura, why not tell me?"

"Zie begged me not too. She really did need to get over you. Her love for you was affecting us."

"So you're both hoping to start a family?"

"It's on hold for now. I need more time."

"She's a manipulator. She used you to get to me."

"How dare you."

"You're too far gone to see it."

"You're an arrogant ass sometimes."

"I dated her, Laura. I know Zie very well. I know her M.O."

"You're wrong. She loves me."

"So you're meeting her for dinner?"

She gave a nod.

"Pass on a message to her from me."

Her shrug told me she would.

"Tell Zie that if she every contacts me or my family again, which includes Mia, I'll have a restraining order placed on her."

"You're an insensitive bastard, Cameron."

"Really?"

"Yes, you are."

"You can't see it, Laura."

"See what?"

"You made both me and Mia vulnerable. An intolerable mistake."

"How?"

"Zie used her pussy to get to me. And you let her."

"Actually, I seduced her."

"Yes, I'm sure it seemed that way."

She glared. "Zie and I are perfect together."

"Good to hear. Now tell your pussy partner to get her kitty cat claws out of my back or I will personally declaw her. And it will be bloody."

Silence creeped in and backed me up with its intensity.

Laura stared at me. "I'll tell Zie to back off."

"I appreciate that."

"I'm sorry, Cameron. I should never have had that session. I don't know what I was thinking."

"Better," I said. "Are you ready to run this place?"

"Yes," she whispered. "Cameron...forgive me."

"She better not hurt you."

"You still care about me after what I did?"

"I can handle Zie." I scrunched up the receipt and threw it back in the trash. "The question is, can you?"

She looked stunned.

"I'll always be here for you," I reassured her. "Just remember she's dangerous."

"I love her."

"Call me. Anytime. We can share war stories."

CHAPTER 25

MASQUERADE MASKS WERE worn by everyone.

The vibrancy of a Chrysalis party was well underway, with our guests donning the usual attire. Even some of the women dared to wear half corsets, with their masters by their sides. Now and again the roles reversed, with women leading men on thin chains.

From up here on the top step of Chrysalis's staircase, Richard and I both sat side by side, surveying the guests who continued to trickle in, and those who had mingled within the foyer before setting off to explore. There would be plenty for them to see tonight—everything from dungeon play, the spanking rooms, and even a private tour of the stables.

Richard and I too had worn our finest bespoke black tie suits, our masks secured, that usual anticipation rising...

The dramatic notes of a soprano singing Richard's favorite opera, La Traviata by Giuseppe Verdi, carried from the great hall. How I loved this complex, brilliant man with a penchant for danger and the most forgiving heart of anyone I knew, other than Mia, of course.

With him by my side, I'd ruled this empire with a fierce control. The irony was not lost on me that the function of Chrysalis was to offer a safe and secure place in which complete surrender could be realized and freedom from selfhood guaranteed.

A sanctuary for the sexually elite.

Shay had increased the security and no one was getting in

unless he personally sanctioned it.

Our attention was momentarily pulled to that passionate couple to the left of the stairs, their wild lovemaking against the wall having drawn a small audience.

The mood sent a crackling electricity through the air.

No one could throw a party like us. Even a few of our leather clad ponies had been set free for the evening and allowed to wander among the guests. Their tails were made out of real horsehair, and their erections stood as proud as the men who wore them. Some held hands, while others wove in and out of the crowd, making new friends and hugging old ones.

An hour ago I'd gathered my staff and delivered the news I was leaving. Most had taken it well. Though not Penny, Scarlet, or Lotte. They'd begged me to change my mind. This was not how things were meant to go.

We all knew that.

I'd created this safe haven for other likeminded members and the director leaving was unfathomable. Life had a funny way of changing plans right after you'd made them.

Chrysalis, an avant garde lifestyle I could no longer partake in.

I'd given my final order to Scarlet and Lotte—

"Prepare Mia."

They'd led her away and right now she'd be immersed in a sensual pampering in the spa, and, afterward, binding her in fine chains using Shibari.

Richard patted my back. "We've had some fun times, haven't we?"

"The best."

"I'm going to miss you, Cam."

"Come visit."

"You bet."

"You do realize what you pulled off for me, don't you?"

"You keep reminding me."

"You saved us."

"Yeah, well you saved me. We'll be waiting for you."

Now, more than ever, I realized how much I needed tonight. Mia had foreseen that leaving here wouldn't be easy.

"You know what impressed me the most?" said Richard.

I turned to face him.

"Even after you believed I'd purposely lost all your money you still didn't hate me. That was enlightening."

"Apparently lack of sleep doesn't look good on me."

He leaned against me for a second. "Losing your friendship would crush me."

"Never going to happen, buddy."

"Dominic's not taking it well."

"Look after him."

"Of course."

I reached into my pocket and withdrew the gold key, a symbol of all I held dear, and handed it to him.

A smile slid across his face. "Never thought the day would come."

The crowd mingled and the erotic tension rose. These stunning men and women would soon be immersed in everything from edge play, bondage, and public displays of affection that went beyond the ordinary.

I really was going to miss it.

"The Harrington Suite was always destined to be for the three of us," he said softly.

"I know."

"You haven't been in there since you caught Zie…"

He was kind enough not to say the word orgy.

"Actually, I gave Mia a peek during her first tour," I said.

"Interesting."

"Mia wants this."

He patted my back. "It may well be her last chance. Next thing you'll be running for office."

"Hardly. My hands are going to be full."

Richard fiddled with his cufflink. "Shay's taking the night off."

"Yes."

"Will he be in there?" he said. "Watching you?"

"No."

Shay had selected a small crowd of doms and their subs to be present. Nothing too intimidating. Men and women who I had profiled and worked with over the years. My trust in their loyalty was solidified, and in their ability to know what was expected from them during a session when it was a sub's first time on show.

"This session with her," I said. "Now that it's here..."

"The art of the performance," said Richard softly. "Proving just how sacred sex really is."

"I don't want you in there, Richard."

"I'm actually planning on a threesome."

My gaze snapped to his. "Shay and Arianna?"

"You're my inspiration."

"Let Shay win sometimes."

"I'll take it under consideration." He nodded toward the foyer. "Here's your girl."

Blinking into the darkened foyer, I spotted that iron cage being wheeled through, my submissive locked inside and stunningly bound in fine gold chains over her naked body. Her face was masked and her eyes scanned the crowd. Perhaps looking for me.

I patted Richard's shoulder.

And then re-secured my mask.

Pushing myself to my feet and descending the stairs, I took my time to savor this ritual of initiating a new submissive.

The entourage of ten doms, all wearing tuxes and masks, led the way into the vast ballroom that was the Harrington Suite.

The cage was lifted up and placed on a low table in the center. There was a womblike feel in here, with the drapes drawn and the deep red lighting flooding down from the long line of chandeliers.

Although aware of the small crowd who took their place not that far away, my focus rested on Mia. Beneath these lights, she looked ethereal—a stunning vision of blonde locks and beautiful eyes hiding behind a mask.

I approached her. "Told you I'd get you in a cage."

Her gaze flittered toward the others—all ten masters with their subs now sitting at their feet. All of them seasoned, quiet, and respectful.

Song of Sophia by Dead Can Dance oozed from hidden speakers, turning the heat up on this splendorous erotic tension.

Mia's fingers tightened around the bars.

"Keep your eyes on me, Mia."

To the left, a velvet drape hung over the table, and upon it was a selection of the toys I'd be using. That violet wand was ready to deliver high voltage sensations for sensual pain play, and that multi-speed wand was plugged in and ready. There were nipple clamps, and my favorite—labia chains to completely expose Mia and showcase the beauty of her sex.

We weren't there yet.

I needed her tranced out, forgetting her surroundings, uncaring of voyeurs. The ultimate desired result was Mia so aroused she'd yearn to be watched coming.

And coming again. Wanting to share her profound experience.

The eyes peering through those masks revealed most of the masters had tranced out. The subs at their feet were equally aroused, their nipples hard buds of desire, and more than likely wishing they were the ones confined.

I gestured for Mia to turn around. "Let's begin."

She gave a nod as I took my time to ease the Shibari chains off her. They'd need to come off for this next part. I threw them onto the table with a clang.

Her butt cheeks pressed against the bars as I reached for the violet wand, brought it over, and caressed her left buttock. She flinched when I delivered a jolt. Working around her body, I lulled her, seeing the release of endorphins flooding her, indicated by her blue eyes sparkling and pupils dilating. Her bliss had heighted from the way she eased into the movement—this dance of bondage she fell into naturally.

I shrugged out of my jacket and threw it on the table. "Stand up."

She did as I commanded.

Her vulnerability, her surrender, stirred my desire and made my cock ache for her. Reaching through and around her hips, I grabbed her butt, dug my fingernails in, and pulled her until her sex rested close between the bars.

Our eyes met. "Here's your reward, kitten."

Her head fell back. Locks tumbled as my mouth met her clit and suckled. The tip of my tongue strummed her.

When I broke away, Mia let out a protracted moan.

"What does the cage represent, Mia?"

"My complete surrender, Master."

Rewarding her answer with delicate flicks of my tongue on her clit, I brought her closer again.

"And?" I asked.

"I'm willing to give up my freedom for you." Her fingers

intertwined in my hair, clutching my head against her.

I broke away and stared up at her.

Her expression shifted as her eyes darted toward our voyeurs.

A flitter of eyelids, a nervous flush on her chest. *Doubt.*

She wasn't ready. Not really.

I was her master, her lover, and the man she trusted above all.

I didn't want her to feel she'd not lived up to my expectations. I didn't care if they were here or not. For me this scene had been played out so many times it had lost its potency.

A wave of my hand gave the order.

They were to leave now, give us the privacy Mia needed and I craved.

Besides, I preferred to have her all to myself.

I removed my mask and placed it on the table.

With them gone and the click of the door being locked, I looked back at her. "I'm going to do things to you that I don't want them to witness." It was a small lie, but I hoped a comforting one nonetheless.

"Oh?"

"I refuse to give away any of my secrets." I reached out. "Mask."

She pulled it off her face handed it to me. "What are you going to do to me?"

I needed to get her back into subspace.

"This." I reached out and slipped two fingers along her sex and slid them into her. "Bounce."

Dutifully she obeyed. Her hands wrapped around the bars, her knuckles went white, and she sank onto my fingers. Her head fell back and cascading locks whipped behind her.

"Slower," I ordered.

"Yes, sir," she said, her hips rising and falling, thighs shuddering. My fingers delivered the kind of pleasure a good sub deserved. My thumb circled her clit.

I withdrew my hand. "Too fast, Mia. You know how I feel about obedience."

"I'll go slower, sir," she promised breathlessly.

Opening the cage door, I gestured for her to near. "No. You have to earn the right to come out."

Mia pressed her face between the bars and pointed. "That one, master."

She had chosen the large white wand and I gave a nod she'd earned it. With a flick of button came that fast buzz, the power tool of vibrators, and her eyes widened with excitement.

Caressing her nipples with the rounded end, I watched them harden. The scent of her arousal caused my cock to twinge and press against my pants.

My need to see her fulfilled forced me to control both myself and her.

"Hands behind your back," I demanded.

She gave a quick nod as she clasped her hands low at the base of her spine. Her hips arched toward me and her need screamed in her heavy lidded eyes.

"Please, master," she begged.

I placed the vibrator on the table and turned it off.

She looked forsaken.

"Do you trust me, Mia?"

"Yes, sir."

"Good." I brought over that delicate thin string belt. Hanging from each end were three small metal clamps, and I wrapped the chain around her waist and brought the ends toward her sex. Taking my time, I fastened those clamps to her outer labia, and then gently eased her folds back to completely expose her. Her swollen clitoris was now viewable from any angle, and it shone from the way I'd coated that small nub with her wetness.

Her thighs shuddered and her small gasps were audible. Her gaze flit out to where that crowd had once stood, as though fantasizing they were here.

"Good girl." I closed the cage door.

Reaching back for the vibrator, I fired it up, then I gestured for Mia's pussy to be presented and gave a stern nod of approval when she did.

She let out a protracted moan when the massaging head thrummed against her clit, pounding her, sending shockwaves of pleasure.

"Yes," she said in a rush.

"Who do you belong to, Mia?"

"You, sir."

"You've been a very good girl tonight."

"Thank you, sir."

"What do good girls get?"

"To come, Master."

"That is correct."

I lowered the wand against her entrance and raised it to rub her clit, sweeping it over that exposed pussy, letting it rebound. I pressed firmly, lighter when she neared—teasing, controlling. Her inner thighs grew soaking wet and her hips rocked.

"Remain still," I ordered firmly.

"Yes sir, sorry sir."

"Good girl. Is that nice, Mia?"

She gazed down at the vibrator, long lashes fluttering with her closeness. "I like it."

She ran her hand over her nipple, licked her lips in a sensuous tease, and looked at me with love in her gaze.

"Hands, Mia," I snapped. "Obey."

She clasped them behind her, her hips thrusting insistently, her eyes begging for release.

"Answer me this," I whispered up at her. "Get it right and you'll be allowed to come."

Her frown deepened.

"What does la petite mort mean?"

She stuttered out, "It's a French euphemism for orgasm."

"Good. Now show me what it means."

"Yes, sir." Thighs shaking, body trembling, her moans echoed as her climax riveted her.

I let her come down slowly, breathlessly.

"You like your cage, Mia?"

She barely managed a nod.

Lifting her out, I let her catch her breath and find her footing.

"You refuse to answer?" I turned her around and bent her over the table, delivering spank after spank to her buttocks.

"Sorry, sir." She wiggled. "I love my cage."

"Good to hear." I rested my back against the table and pulled her to my chest and she stood on her tiptoes before me. Her back was pressed to my front as she faced the room. After placing my cock at her entrance, I eased her down over my shaft.

She let out a long sigh, as though only now settling.

That silver chain hung low over her hips and those clamps still gently eased her labia apart, making her sex spectacularly accessible.

Mia trembled with excitement.

"Slow your breathing," I warned.

She gave a nod she'd try.

"This final test is to gauge your ability to show self-control, Mia. Are you ready?"

"Yes, sir."

I buried deeper inside her and her hands naturally found their way behind her back, offering the pose of a sub, letting me know she was ready.

"When I say begin," I told her. "Circle your hips slowly and pause when you've completed a full circle. Push your pelvis out a little and wait. You'll be well rewarded if you obey."

Mia completed her first circle. Her hips nudged forward and she paused. I clasped the handle of the vibrator, brought it over, and tapped the rounded head on one of her nipples then the other.

Her pussy tightened and flinched around me.

It felt fucking amazing.

Concentrating, I pulled myself back from the edge. "Again."

Another circle, and this time her reward was the vibrator pressed on her clit. She threw her head back and short, sharp gasps escaped her.

"Concentrate," I chastised. "The movement must be fluid. A continuous circling, a brief pause, and then another circle."

Another reward.

Within seconds Mia fell into her stride, her hips moving effortlessly. A soft sigh escaped when I delivered her present of that powerful vibrator. My left arm held her around the waist as I rocked into her. Her trembling hinted she'd perhaps not quite make another rotation—

But she did. Her desire to please warmed my heart, forcing my hand to hold the wand permanently between her thighs—

Merciful…

Mia shuddered, squeezed, and awaited my permission.

I refused to give it.

I needed to push her farther than I ever had, needed her to know she was capable of surrendering to a profound pleasure. Her consciousness would expand until her mind let her go and her heart soared to the level of bliss she was capable of.

Time slipped away.

Her slow steady cycles continued. Each time her hips thrust forward, her momentary pause was rewarded with the ecstasy delivered to her clit, and then I again lifted the wand away from her and waited for Mia to complete another circling of her hips.

Her body trembled. Her breaths were short and sharp.

Eventually, I pressed the vibrator firmly there.

And kept it there.

"You may come, sub," I demanded.

She screamed her climax and I clutched her to me, holding her through her endless climax.

Nuzzling into her neck, I whispered, "I'm about to fuck you so hard, sub, you'll forget your own name."

Grabbing Mia up then easing her down on the table, I took my time to remove those clamps and throw them. Climbing onto her, I grasped her hands above her head to pin her down before thrusting deep.

I rode her into oblivion, pounding her violently, my hips thrusting hard as the sound of flesh striking flesh resonated over the music.

She shook her head from side to side, all golden locks and flushed skin. Her moan grew uncontrollable.

With a firm kiss, my tongue fucked her just as hard. Our tongues battled—me for control and hers yearning for it. Her back arched as I filled her with warmth, and I too fell, and fell, and fell, until the room disappeared and all I knew was her.

Refusing to pull out of her, I needed these minutes that followed for my equilibrium to right again. Both of us were covered in perspiration and smeared in this delicious mess of our perfect tryst.

Mia blinked up at me. "I'm speechless."

"That's a nice change."

She gave my arm a playful punch. "That was amazing."

I arched a brow. "For the record, this new memory surpasses them all, Ms. Lauren."

My head was filled with her, only her.

She'd been the only woman who could heal me, reach me, and now I knew that Mia was the only woman who could've ever broken me out of my very own Chrysalis.

My lips met hers as I gave a silent prayer of thanks for her being mine.

CHAPTER 26

A SUNSET LIT up the west.

Oranges and reds spread in a blast of color, and I couldn't wait for Mia to see it.

For now though, her eyes were shielded by that black velvet blindfold, her hands clasped in her lap.

The BMW hummed as we swept along the 90, getting closer.

It was good to leave formality behind, if only for a while. Both of us wore jeans and T-shirts, though with the top down we also wore our jackets to hold off the chill.

Mia turned her head toward me. "How about now?"

"You really need to learn some patience, Ms. Lauren."

"And you need to stop being so secretive."

"It's a surprise. It's meant to be fun."

She gasped. "Did the word *fun* just come out of Cameron Cole's mouth?"

"Careful."

"I'm serious. This is progress."

"Do you want to be spanked?"

She bit her lip, lowered her chin, and that served as her answer.

I reached over and squeezed her hand. "Guess what?"

"We're going to sleep together tonight."

"As long as I have that, Mia, life is pretty fantastic."

She sighed with happiness.

"New York's a great place to study fashion," I said.

"Or business."

I flashed her a smile, despite knowing she couldn't see it. "As soon as we get settled, I can arrange for you to interview at some of the top fashion houses."

"Your dad's offered me an intern position."

"So I hear."

"I'm considering it."

"I may have an opening in my department. Right up there on the top floor of Cole Tower. It's an impressive view. I'm looking for a dynamic recruit willing to take on extracurricular activities."

"Which will include?"

"Being available at all times to consult with me on sensitive issues."

"Such as?"

"You think I'm suggesting an executive assistant who I can throw over my desk?"

She giggled. "When can I start?"

"You'd have the option of moving into marketing."

"So you can control the advertising?"

"Or you can become my executive advisor."

"Would I get a car?"

"How about a helicopter? You can commute with me."

"Oh my God."

I smiled. "We'll make it work."

"Will I get an office?"

"If you like."

"Near yours?"

"Most definitely."

I steered us around a tight curve and she leaned into the turn.

"I'll get to see you during the day," she said. "My dream job."

Glancing over, I was reassured she truly looked forward to this and I was comforted with the thought she'd be close. What I wanted more than anything was for her to be happy. "Don't ever give up on your dream, Mia."

"Scarlet told me that with you the world is my oyster."

I took her hand. "You don't need me for that to be true."

Her frown line deepened and something told me she was thinking of us, our future, and where that might lead her. We'd both been faced with such profound changes lately and in many ways we were still reeling.

My once reluctance to take up the challenge of running Cole Tea gripped me with the fierceness of a maddening fugue. I had surrendered to my future, and with Mia by my side I knew anything was possible. Taking the business to the next level filled me with the kind of passion I never realized I was capable of.

"I'm happy you're coming with me," I said. "I don't take it for granted."

"Silly." She reached out and her hand rested on my thigh. "Where are we going today?"

I chuckled. "Life is a journey. Enjoy it."

She settled back and sighed contentedly. Seeing her relaxed and feeling safe warmed my heart and brought the peace I yearned for.

Arriving at our destination, I pulled off the road.

She shifted in her seat, sensing we'd arrived, her excitement tangible.

After parking, I took a moment to savor this, making sure I remembered every single second of being here with her.

I strolled around to her side and held the door open.

A seagull flew over us and I watched Mia's expression, her fingertips trailing over the edge of the velvet blindfold. She breathed in the fresh air.

I knew she'd guess our location from the yachts shifting on their mores and the lapping water.

A couple of pedestrians strolled past us and reacted when they saw Mia's blindfold. Two kids on bikes whizzed by.

Taking Mia by the hand, I guided her toward the harbor and we made our way along the wharf.

"Ha! I know where we are."

"Silence, Ms. Lauren."

My life had changed irrevocably the moment I'd met her. Her sweetness, her love had been what I'd needed all along. Before her I'd spent my days dedicated to making those around me happy, and some part of me had doubted I deserved that same contentment.

She was the greatest reward, but I knew we couldn't continue like this. Change lingered in the air. And I welcomed it, craved it.

There, secured at the end, was my 57m Remington RIO luxury

yacht, once named La Ricochet. This boat, along with the rest of my life, was going to be transported to our new home in the Hamptons. A quick helicopter ride from Cole Tower.

And there it would stay, right up until the moment the Cole skyscraper was completed in Los Angeles, and we'd be able to move back.

For now, we'd be calling New York home.

Mia leaned against me and nuzzled into my chest. She fit so perfectly there. This meeting of minds and hearts was more then I'd ever imagined possible.

"Ready, Mia?"

She nodded.

I eased off her blindfold and tucked it into my pocket.

She squealed. "Are we going out on it?"

I grinned at her. "Mia…look at the name."

"The name?"

I gestured toward the starboard—

It was then she saw the boat's new moniker.

The Mrs.

Her hands cupped her mouth.

Kneeling before her, I brought out the small black box. "Mia Lauren." I lifted its lid. "Will you marry me?"

A breeze caught her hair, brushing it over her face.

It made her giggle.

I beamed up at her. "Now's a good time to answer."

"Yes, of course. Yes, yes, yes, oh Cameron, *yes.*"

I slid the ring onto her finger.

Her eyes widened in wonder at the elegant Asscher cut diamond.

She fell into my arms and I lifted her, laughing and spinning her around, feeling freer then I ever had and marveling that I'd found her.

I carried her along the dock, up the short steps, and onto the yacht.

Up and onto the upper deck.

The captain navigated *The Mrs.* out of the harbor and guided us out along the coast. The water, still like glass, reflecting the moon as we cut through. The boat left its transient mark.

Mia and I ate dinner and spent the rest of the evening dancing to R&B and jazz and endlessly talking. She might have talked more than me, but I loved every second of it.

Snuggled together, we leaned on the balustrade and savored the setting sun.

Our future looked something like that sunset, profoundly stunning, an array of scattered colors, a ray path of brilliant light in all its oranges and reds, melting on the horizon.

I believed this was really what Carl Jung meant about how nature thinks—that no matter how much pain we endure in life, if we wait long enough, eventually we'll find our way back to a place where we're no longer running and can find our center again.

Find ourselves.

A moment to just be.

ABOUT THE AUTHOR

Vanessa Fewings is the award-winning author of the Enthrall Sessions.

Vanessa is also the author of The Stone Masters Vampire Series, a paranormal saga.

Her romantic comedy, Piper Day's Ultimate Guide to Avoiding George Clooney, has already garnered a buzz of excitement from readers around the world. Prior to publishing, Vanessa worked as a registered nurse and midwife. She holds a Masters Degree in Psychology. She has traveled extensively throughout the world and has lived in Germany, Hong Kong, and Cyprus.

Born and raised in England, Vanessa now proudly calls herself an American and resides in California with her husband.

Other books in the series:

Enthrall
Enthrall Her
Enthrall Him

Novellas
Cameron's Control
Cameron's Contract
Richard's Reign

Printed in Great Britain
by Amazon.co.uk, Ltd.,
Marston Gate.